MACE

LIGHTHOUSE SECURITY & INVESTIGATIONS

MARYANN JORDAN

Mace (Lighthouse Security Investigations) Copyright 2018

All rights reserved. No part of this book may be reproduced or transmitted in any form or by any means, electronic or mechanical, including photocopying, recording, or by any information storage and retrieval system without the written permission of the author, except where permitted by law.

If you are reading this book and did not purchase it, then you are reading an illegal pirated copy. If you would be concerned about working for no pay, then please respect the author's work! Make sure that you are only reading a copy that has been officially released by the author.

This book is a work of fiction. Names, characters, places, and incidents either are products of the author's imagination or are used fictitiously. Any resemblance to actual persons, living or dead, events, or locales is entirely coincidental.

Cover Design by: Becky McGraw

Editor: Shannon Brandee Eversoll

Proofreader: Myckel Anne Phillips

ISBN: print: 978-1-947214-28-6

❊ Created with Vellum

ACKNOWLEDGMENTS

First and foremost, I have to thank my husband, Michael. Always believing in me and wanting me to pursue my dreams, this book would not be possible without his support. To my daughters, MaryBeth and Nicole, I taught you to follow your dreams and now it is time for me to take my own advice.

My best friend, Tammie, who for over twenty years has been with me through thick and thin. You've filled the role of confidant, supporter, and sister.

My other best friend, Myckel Anne, who keeps me on track, keeps me grounded, and most of all – keeps my secrets. Thank you for not only being my proofreader and my Marketing PA, but friend. I do not know what I would do without you in my life.

My beta readers kept me sane, cheered me on, found all my silly errors, and often helped me understand my characters through their eyes. A huge thank you to Denise, Sandi, Barbara, Jennifer, Danielle, Tracey, Lynn,

Stracey, and Jamila for being my beta girls who love alphas!

Shannon Brandee Eversoll as my editor and Myckel Anne Phillips as my proofreader gave their time and talents to making all my books as well written as it can be.

My street team, Jordan Jewels, you all are amazing! You volunteer your time to promote my books and I cannot thank you enough! I hope you will stay with me, because I have lots more stories inside, just waiting to be written!

My PA Barbara keeps me going when I feel overwhelmed and I am so grateful for not only her assistance, but her friendship.

Chas…thank you for all you do!

Most importantly, thank you readers. You allow me into your home for a few hours as you disappear into my characters and you support me as I follow my indie author dreams.

AUTHOR INFORMATION

USA TODAY BESTSELLING AND AWARD WINNING AUTHOR

I am an avid reader of romance novels, often joking that I cut my teeth on the historical romances. I have been reading and reviewing for years. In 2013, I finally gave into the characters in my head, screaming for their story to be told. From these musings, my first novel, Emma's Home, The Fairfield Series was born.

I was a high school counselor having worked in education for thirty years. I live in Virginia, having also lived in four states and two foreign countries. I have been married to a wonderfully patient man for thirty-seven years. When writing, my dog or one of my four cats can generally be found in the same room if not on my lap.

Please take the time to leave a review of this book.

Feel free to contact me, especially if you enjoyed my book. I love to hear from readers!

Facebook

Email
Website

As a child, my parents took our family on a vacation to Maine. I remember how different the beaches were and was fascinated with the rough, rocky coastline. That memory stayed in my mind as I tried to decide on a location for my new series.
So, to my parents, who always tried to show my brother and I new places, filled with new sights and sounds, I dedicate this book.

1

The lights were low, the room illuminated only by the flicker of the flame from the lantern. The rain outside pounded against the window, and the waves could be heard crashing against the rocks down below. The living room in the old house was small, holding a worn sofa against the front wall near the windows. A rocking chair, with a green padded cushion, was angled next to the unlit fireplace and another chair facing the sofa, its seat cushions sagging from years of use. An end table next to the sofa held a brass lamp, but with the electricity out, it became merely an ornament.

An old man sat in the chair, leaning forward with his forearms resting on his knees. His bushy white eyebrows lifted and lowered as his blue eyes pierced the only other person in the room.

His voice, like gravel, said, "Even his own men called him a maniac. He was cruel, make no mistake about that. He once made a commander eat his own sliced off ears sprinkled with salt before he killed him. It's said he once made someone eat the heart of another before killing him as well. They even say he burned a cook alive, saying he was a greasy fellow who would fry well." Chuckling, "He made the other Edward, Blackbeard, look like a schoolboy."

His listener sat on a low stool, his eyes large as his heart pounded in his chest, attention focused on the old man. Barely breathing, he was afraid the very sound of inhaling would call forth the ghosts from the past.

"Born in London, he was, to a family mostly of thieves. He eventually crossed the sea to come to the New World, settling in Boston. He raided up and down the New England coast, attacking ships, robbing every vessel he came across. He stole all the way down to the Caribbean. It seemed like nothing could stop him and his terror on the sea. Some say his boat sank in a storm, and that's what killed him. But others say he died after being set adrift by one of the crews when they mutinied against him. Others say he was rescued by a French ship, but when they found out who he was, they hung him."

The old man leaned forward and asked, "You scared yet?" His laugh rumbled deep in his chest, "Ned Lowe lived a long time ago, boy. No need to be scared of him now."

Ten-year-old Mason Hanover sucked in a deep breath before letting it out slowly, willing his heartbeat to slow. "Wasn't there any good in him at all, Grampa?"

"Well, it appears that when he first got to Boston he married a woman, but she died giving birth to their only child. Even though the child lived, they say the loss of his wife had a profound effect on him. He never forced married men to join his crew and always allowed women to return to port safely if they happened to be on a ship that he was piratin'."

Mason shivered despite the warmth, the summer storm outside still raging. As scared as he was, he loved sitting in his grandfather's small house perched on the rocks overlooking the sea. About the only thing he loved more was when Grampa took him out on his boat, and they explored many of the coves up and down the coast where they lived.

"Who are you going to tell about next, Grampa?"

"How about I tell you some tales of lighthouse keepers...some true life heroes?"

Grinning widely, he nodded, his enthusiasm evident on his face.

"Well, Marcus Hanna lived in the mid-1800's and was a lighthouse keeper famous for his heroism. He's the only person in history to be honored with both the Medal of Honor and the Gold Lifesaving Medal."

"His name sounds a lot like mine."

Nodding, Grampa said, "Yeah, it does."

"What'd he do?"

"His father was the keeper of the Franklin Island Light, right here in Maine. Marcus spent his young years working with his pops before he went off to sea when he was only ten years old—"

"Ten years old? That's how old I am! He went off to sea?" he exclaimed, his eyes wide with surprise.

Nodding, Grampa said, "Things were different back

then, son. Men became men a lot earlier than now." Continuing, he said, "He enlisted when the Civil War broke out and served in the Navy for a year and then was mustered out to various regiments. He once volunteered to carry water behind enemy lines to the rest of his company. With the worst fighting taking place all around him, he took care of his fellow soldiers. That's when he got the Medal of Honor."

Mason sat up straighter, his gaze stuck to his grandfather, thinking of the brave soldier. "Do you think he was scared?"

"Only a fool isn't scared, boy," Grampa answered. "But a hero is one who acts in spite of bein' scared."

He nodded silently, thinking that he would like to be a soldier one day. A bolt of lightning slashed through the sky, illuminating the room through the windows. He jumped as the loud thunder cracked and the little house shook. His eyes wide, he looked around, hoping the house would still be standing when the storm passed.

"Don't you worry," Grampa said. "This house has stood for a hundred years, right here on this spot. No storm's gonna bring it down."

He nodded, believing his grandfather. He watched as the older man took a swig of his coffee from the old enameled cup he always drank from. He liked it here in his grandfather's house, where everything was the same. Day in and day out, he knew exactly what he would find when he was here. So different from his own home.

"Get to the good stuff, Grampa!"

Chuckling again, a deep cough racked his body, and

he had to wait a minute until his breathing eased. Clearing his throat, he said, "After the war, he took after his pops and became a lighthouse keeper. One night, he risked his life saving two sailors who had wrecked on the rocks below. He braved freezing temperatures in a blizzard, throwing a line to the ship. He got both sailors off their ship and got them to safety."

"Is that when he got the next medal?"

"Yes. He got the Gold Lifesaving Medal then. He's the only person in history to get both of those awards. One military and one civilian for heroism."

Wide-eyed again, Mason leaned forward listening to every word. He had not realized it, but the worst of the storm outside had passed, leaving only the rain still hitting the windows. Biting his lip nervously, he asked, "It's still raining mighty hard, Grampa. Do you think it'd be okay if I stayed here tonight?"

His grandfather settled his piercing blue eyes onto him, nodding slowly. They both knew the real reason he wanted to stay was that his parents were either fighting or drinking. Maybe both.

His sister was spending the night with their aunt, and he did not want to be at home alone when his parents were fighting.

"Yeah, boy. I think you'd get too wet if you tried to go outside now. You can bed down with me tonight, and I'll get you home tomorrow."

An hour later, he was snuggled under the covers on the cot in his grandfather's bedroom. His grandmother had passed away two years earlier, but he still remembered the joy he felt when he was able to spend the night with them. Their house on the cliffs overlooking the ocean was small but cozy.

The quilt, pulled up underneath his chin, was soft and one of his favorites. It had been made by his grandmother many, many years before. She had taken old scraps cut from clothing long worn out, and made a quilt covered in boats. The bright colors were now faded, but it provided all the warmth that he needed... along with his memories of her.

The rain against the bedroom window was now just drizzle, comforting, rather than scary. His grandfather, having finished in the bathroom, walked into the bedroom. Placing his glasses on the nightstand, he walked over to the cot, kneeling on the floor.

"You say your prayers yet?"

"I was waiting for you, Grampa."

His grandfather nodded his head, laid his large, rough, gnarled hand on his, and they bowed together. After a prayer of thanks for the day and safety for all those out on the sea, he got to his feet.

His Grampa started to walk toward the bed, when he turned back and looked down on him. "I didn't scare you too bad talking about the pirates, did I?"

Mason looked up at the wise, old face he loved so dearly, and shook his head. "Nah, I wasn't too scared, Grampa. I know pirates lived a long time ago, so even if they were bad people, they're not here anymore."

"That's right. Pirates are long dead, for many years now."

"They were really bad people, Grampa. I'm glad we don't have anybody like that anymore."

His grandfather's face twisted for a moment, as though struggling with what to say. Sighing heavily, he finally said, "I suppose you're not too young to know that there are still bad people in the world. They might not be pirates like Ned Lowe, but there are still some really bad people in the world. You gotta watch out for them, and you gotta protect other people you love from them as well. Just like Marcus Hanna...there're all kinds of rescuers and you can be just like that. A real lighthouse keeper in the truest sense...a rescuer."

Lying in his cot long after his grandfather began to snore, he thought of what Grampa had said. Bad people in the world, watching out for them, protecting others. He didn't know what his grandfather meant, but lying in the still of the night, he vowed to do just that...be a Keeper.

Six Years Later

The small boat rocked upon the waves, but Mason handled the craft expertly. Moving along the rocky shoreline, he kept his eyes peeled for the caves he knew were hidden among the rocks.

His grandfather had shown him where some of the caves lay, a few nothing more than a small indentation in the stone, but as he continued to explore he found at least one that was much bigger. Underneath the old

Maker's Point Lighthouse were caves that had been naturally formed, and possibly dug out even more, many years ago. His grandfather had told him tales of pirates hiding treasure and, as a young boy, he had been excited to look for some.

He accepted that the treasures didn't exist now, but still loved to explore their depths along the rocky shore.

Checking his watch, he decided that he needed to get back home soon. He had promised his sister he would help with her chores before their mother got home. Their father had finally taken off, no longer wanting the responsibilities of fatherhood or marriage. His mother worked long hours at the grocery store in town to make sure they had what they needed.

Coming around the corner of an edge of rocks, his sharp eyes detected the opening of the cave that had long fascinated him. Easy to miss unless you knew what you were looking for, he always found it. Knowing he did not have time to explore it more today, he turned the boat around, heading back home.

His weekends, during the school year, were filled with sports, homework, and working at the same grocery store as his mother. Grateful it was now summer, he knew he could come back tomorrow.

Once home, he quickly put away the boat and headed up the path to the small house, where his Grampa lived. After their father took off for parts unknown, they were unable to keep the house they had lived in. Grampa said he was happy to have them, so now his mom and his sister shared one of the tiny upstairs rooms, and he had the other to himself.

He did not mind since he had his own place and it was quiet. His clothes hung on pegs along the wall, his bed pushed next to another wall, directly under the window. The only other furniture in the room was a small table with a lamp on top and a shelf underneath that held his books.

He moved to the kitchen, where his sister, Mary, was stirring a pot. "Whatcha got?"

"One of the ladies from the church brought over some stew, so I'm heating it up. Mom said she'd bring home some of that good, thick bread from the grocery store and we can have that with it."

He sighed, knowing that charity might not often come their way, but it did come. He wished it did not bother him that people looked at his family as something to be pitied. *One day, when I'm all grown, I'll make sure Mom and sis have everything they need.*

Mary, with her long brown hair tied with a ribbon at the base of her neck, turned and looked at him. "Are you going to the caves tomorrow?"

He grinned and nodded. "Yeah. Thought I'd do a little more exploring in one of the big ones I found, near the lighthouse."

She smiled back at him before turning to the stove, continuing her stirring. "Those caves scare me. I bet they're full of bats and spiders and—"

"No. No. They might have a couple of bats in them, but not many at all. And I've never seen a spider. They're mostly clean, and this one's big. It goes pretty far back I think, but I haven't explored it all the way."

"I swear, I think you'd like to live there," she said.

He heard their mother driving up in the driveway and pulled down the bowls from the cabinets and set them near the stove. Mary had already moved to the door to greet her, while he stood thinking about her last comment, and the reality hit him. *Yeah, I think I would like to live in one of those big caves.*

That night, as he slept on the cot in his small room with the moonlight shining through the window over his bed, he dreamed of having his own house by the water before it morphed into the deep, cavernous spaces underneath.

2

FIFTEEN YEARS LATER

The lone man stood at the top of the lighthouse, his muscular forearms leaning on the rail, his hands clasped together. His head was bowed, giving the appearance that he was at prayer. His dark hair whipped about in the wind and as he lifted his gaze, staring out over the sea, his thoughts were as turbulent as the waves crashing against the rocks below.

After inheriting his grandfather's small house and land, he'd purchased the lighthouse, which had no longer been in use, along with the land all around it. With the two properties right next to each other, he was assured of his privacy.

Mace loved this time of day, as the sunrise rose over the water, casting the undulating sea in glimmers. Large ships in the distance glided by, mixed with the local fishermen out for their early morning catch. The seagulls called to each other before swooping into the water for their breakfast.

Pulling himself up to his impressive height, he rolled his shoulders back, stretching out the kinks. His night had been restless, but he had no idea why. He dressed in jeans that molded to his muscular form and a thick, thermal, long sleeve shirt helped to ward off the early morning chill. Stooping, he grabbed his coffee mug from the concrete floor, taking a sip.

As he ran his hand through his dark hair, the ends still slightly damp from his shower, he chuckled, realizing the coffee might warm his insides, but his damp hair still caught the cool breeze.

With a last look at the water, he turned and walked inside. Skirting around the old glass lights, he appreciated the angular prisms set in patterns used for many years to warn seafarers of the rocky shores. He descended the circular stairs, first metal and then concrete, curving around to the bottom of the thirty-foot lighthouse, to where the house was connected. He had redesigned the smaller rooms into spacious living quarters that were open and comfortable.

Walking into the large kitchen, three cats swirled about his ankles, and he looked down, careful to not trip over them. "Haven't they had breakfast yet?"

"You know they have, but with bacon on the stove and biscuits in the oven, cats are just naturally going to want to eat again."

He walked over to the coffee pot and poured another cup. Turning around, he leaned his hip against the counter while sipping the hot, black brew. He watched as Marge flipped the bacon expertly before forking it onto paper towels to soak up the grease.

Marge Tiddle, and her husband, Horace, had been with him for several years, but he had known them for many years before that.

She was slightly plump, her thick gray hair cut just below her ears and her blue eyes just as sharp as they had always been, even though she retired from the CIA five years ago. Wearing a gray *Go Army* sweatshirt and sweatpants, she seemed to blend a combination of Drill Sergeant and den mother all into one.

Pulled from an Army Special Forces mission and tasked to work on a CIA special operation, he had met her years before in Afghanistan. Inwardly wincing, as he always did when he thought back to that time, the pain of leaving his squad suddenly, without a chance to say goodbye, gouged deep. Taking another sip of the strong coffee, he was thankful he had been able to reconnect with at least one member of his former squad over a case they were both working on.

"Let go of the past," Marge said, drawing his attention back to her.

Shaking his head while emitting a quick snort, he asked, "How the hell do you get in my head like that?"

Laughing, she replied, "You're easy to read, Mace. I've always been able to read you."

That was certainly true. And probably why she had been looking out for him as long as she had. Even now, with both of them out of the CIA, she made it her job to watch out for him.

Within a few minutes, she served breakfast at the old, wooden table on the other side of the counter. When he built the house, he decided against a formal dining room, expanding the design of the kitchen to include that space.

Horace came through the back door, shutting it quickly behind him, stomping his boots on the rug. Walking past Marge, he kissed her on the cheek before heading to the sink to wash his hands. Even at sixty-seven years old, he was spry, his gray hair still sporting the tight military haircut of his youth. Like his wife, he was as sharp as he had been as a much younger man.

"Glorious day out there," he said. Looking over at Mace, he added, "But I guess you already know that, don't you?"

Nodding while forking the fluffy scrambled eggs into his mouth, he swallowed before acknowledging, "Yeah. From the top, it looks like it's going to be a beautiful day." He finished eating quickly and took his plate and cup over to the sink, rinsing it.

Marge shooed him away, saying, "I've got this." Throwing a pointed look at the large basket sitting on the counter, she added, "You can help by taking that on down."

"No problem," he remarked, hefting the basket into his arms.

With a nod to Marge and Horace, he left the room and walked back down the hall, toward the lighthouse. When he came to the steps leading up, he turned to the opposite side and with a quick flip, opened the panel hidden in the wall. He tapped in a security code first, then stood carefully while the retina scan took place. Placing his hand on a finger scanner, he waited until his digital prints had been taken. A door swung open and he entered, shutting it behind him.

Once inside the elevator, he tapped in another security code and began the descent down. At the bottom, the door opened and he entered a hallway with a single door at the end. Once again going through the motions of the security systems, the final door swung open.

He entered into the cavernous main room of Lighthouse Security Investigations. The walls and ceilings were reinforced with steel beams and panels. The concrete floor, while smooth and solid, retained the original look of the cave. The room, sealed and environmentally protected, contained two walls filled with computer equipment, and stations where several men sat manning the keyboards while staring at the screens.

Specialized printers, processors with high-speed connections, servers, and other computer equipment filled the back wall. The fourth wall held large screens, multiple images flashing upon them. Software tools, specific to each employee, enhanced their ability to organize, access and analyze information.

Several doors opened from the large room, leading to the weapons rooms, bunk rooms, gymnasium, and one set of back stairs that led away from the lighthouse. In the center of the space was a large table, easily able to fit twenty people around, if needed. The only decorations in the utilitarian room were framed photographs of famous lighthouse keepers, known for their bravery, many with Coast Guard ships named after them.

LSI...his dream...his vision...now a reality.

Moving to the table, he set the basket down. Calling

out to the others in the room, he said, "Marge sent breakfast."

Immediately, Rank, Josh, and Drew jumped up, their smiles wide as they hurried over. He grinned as he watched them all put their hands in the basket at the same time. Each taking a huge bite of one of Marge's breakfast biscuits, filled with scrambled eggs, bacon, sausage, and cheese, they moaned in unison.

Tate and Clay were still sitting at their computers, but Tate looked over his shoulder, calling out, "Hey, bring one of those over here."

Not to be forgotten, Clay ordered the same thing. Smiling as Rank brought him one of the filled biscuits, he turned away from his computer as he began eating. "Good God, these are fabulous. How the hell did Marge find the time to learn to cook like a grandma while she worked as a CIA operative?"

Laughing, he said, "She always said she missed good Southern cooking when she was stationed in Africa. So, she made sure she wrote down all of her grandmother's recipes so that when her CIA days were over, she could eat the way she wanted."

The others laughed, then their mirth turned into appreciative groans as they ate more of her breakfast biscuits. The super-sized coffee pot on the back counter was working overtime as the men filled their cups.

"Any word from Blake or Cobb?" Mace asked.

"Blake has confirmed that he's finished with his mission and will be flying back this afternoon," Rank said, washing his biscuit down with hot coffee.

Tate reported, "Cobb's fine. Said he's got a little bit

more to do and then he'll be finished. Hopes to be back in a couple of days."

"Bray said he'll be in later. He was out late last night checking on his mission." Drew watched Mace's eyebrow lift in question and hurried to say, "He reported everything was good. Just out late."

He nodded, and asked, "Walker?"

Rank looked over, "He's off today, helping his sister move."

As Rank spoke, he shifted his eyes to his boss, but Mace shuttered his look. He always told his men that family was important, and for them to do what was needed to take care of family. Turning quickly, he said, "Once you finish eating, we'll have the morning meeting. Ten minutes."

The men were ready quickly and, within a few minutes, they were seated at the large table. Mace nodded toward Josh, indicating for him to start the morning reports.

"I checked in with your buddy, Jack Bryant, of Saints Protection and Investigations. He reported that the identity change mission we worked on a few years ago is now on her honeymoon with one of his men."

Rank commented, a grin on his face, "Seems like we're not only in the security business but can play matchmaker as well."

Chuckles were heard around the room and Mace was unable to keep his lips from curving into a smile. Nodding, he replied, "Good. Glad that one worked out well. We'll keep the communications open with the Saints...we may work with them in the future."

Looking down at his tablet, he added, "For possible new missions, the CIA Director, Ted Silver, has informed me of a situation in Honduras that the CIA is monitoring. It may require intervention from us. He'll let us know within the next several weeks. Jerry Dalton, FBI Director has two possible witnesses that the FBI may need our skills in changing identities for. Currently, we're working on security for a family being threatened by a mob boss who's being indicted, as well as some identity changes for others."

With a nod his way, Tate took over with, "One of those changes is for the college-age daughter of the family being threatened by the mob boss. We've got the rest of the family under security, but for her, we're doing a full identity change. That's all for right now."

"Chatter?"

Drew said, "I've been monitoring local as well as State Police. A lot going on, but nothing right now that appears to need our attention."

"On the national level the chatter is much more extensive, but again, nothing that I see requires LSI," Rank commented.

Leaning back, with his elbows propped on the arms of the chair, his fingers steepled together in front of him, Mace nodded slowly. "Seems like the start to a slow week. But then," he added, "that can always change on a dime."

"Works for me, if it gets busy," Drew announced. The others smiled in agreement.

"Okay," Mace stated, placing his hands on the table as he pushed himself to a stand. "Looks like our meeting for this morning is concluded. Let me know if anything changes. I'll be around."

As everyone dispersed to their assignments, he moved to the far wall and through another door. Down a well-lit hall, past the gym and locker rooms, he moved through another security door shutting it carefully behind him. From here, he entered the caves directly underneath the lighthouse, preserved in their natural state. Careful of the moisture on the stone flooring, he made his way downward, coming to an area where he kept a small rowboat.

Settling inside, he grabbed the oars and waited until the waves washing inside the small cave receded, giving a mighty heave backward with the oars. With his strong muscles, he managed to get past the waves, rowing away from the shore and up the coastline. The wind was brisk, but not very strong. It helped to cool his heated muscles as he worked the oars to move across the water. Rowing, he looked around, always checking to make sure that the rocky entrance to his caves was secure.

Satisfied that no one would ascertain what lay below the lighthouse, he smiled. It had taken five years to build the physical location for Lighthouse Security Investigations, calling in all his markers from trusted sources to safely create the compound in the caves so that it could withstand the test of time.

Turning his face toward the sun, he allowed it to warm his body, before settling his gaze out over the horizon. For now, the ocean was peaceful, but he knew how quickly that could change. Just like with LSI…calm one minute, then turbulent the next.

With a last look around, he turned his boat toward the shore and began rowing back. Once inside, after securing the boat, he moved back up the stairs, through the security doors, and into the compound. He had a small, private office, but found that he usually preferred to do his work in the large area with the others. Perhaps it was the camaraderie from his days in the military, or maybe just the idea of teamwork that had been drilled into him, but he loved the energy emanating from a group of people all working with the same purpose.

Stepping back into the main room, he looked up to see a petite woman with dark, pixie-cut hair, a few highlights in pink framing her face, smiling at the group. Barbara Mabrey, another former CIA operative who was tired of the bureaucracy, jumped at the chance to be a part of the team when he'd told her of his idea for LSI. She immediately offered to be the administrative and logistics manager. He had never asked her why she wanted to leave field work behind, opting instead to work behind the scenes with LSI. He figured her reasons were her own, and he was just damn glad she was there—people always underestimate the time and energy it takes to make an operation like this work. Shaking his head, he grinned at the thought of her self-imposed title, considering she was a jack-of-all-trades.

"Hey, y'all," she called out, her southern roots infusing her words. "Sorry I'm late, traffic was horrible."

Since there was no traffic within 20 miles of their located, he tilted his head, lifting an eyebrow in silent question.

She placed her hands on her lean hips and shrugged

her shoulders. "Well, it was worth a try. To be honest, I just overslept."

"Late night, Babs?" Drew asked, wiggling his eyebrows in a suggestive manner.

She grinned as she wiggled hers right back toward him. "Hell, yeah. Found me a big old southern boy and decided it was time for me to save a horse."

Several of the men groaned and Drew shook his head. "TMI!" he exclaimed, a scowl on his face. A Southerner, like Babs, they shared a tight bond, but he made it clear he did not want to hear about her love life.

"Well, if y'all can talk about your conquests, then certainly I can too!"

Mace cut in, "Right now, I don't want to hear about anyone's love life."

The group chuckled, turning back to their activities. Babs winked at him before moving to her desk, firing up her laptop. She had no problem taking care of the administrative side of the business, even though she was completely qualified for a number of jobs within LSI. She was no longer interested in working in the field, instead, taking on the monumental task of handling everything from the mundane timesheets of the men, to the billing, and all the other administrative necessities of running the agency. Dedicated and discrete, she was the perfect person for the job.

In fact, as Mace looked around the room, he knew that all of his employees, known collectively as The Keepers, were dedicated, discrete, and perfect for their jobs. Former SEALs Rank, Tate, Cobb, and Walker; former Army Ranger Clay; former Army Special Forces

Bray; former Deltas Josh and Blake; former Air Force Special Ops Drew; and, of course, former CIA Babs. If that was all they brought to the table, that would have been enough. But, like himself, they had been recruited and part of the CIA Special Ops before joining his private organization.

All were expert in carrying out what had been deemed deniable covert operations and were trained in sabotage personnel recovery, bomb damage assessment, hostage rescue, and counterterrorism. Each one was smart as hell and tough as nails. And, everyone approached all missions, whether mundane or risky, as worthwhile, sharing in his vision.

Looking back down at his computer, he grinned, knowing LSI was truly built on a rock-solid foundation. "Keep checking the chatter and let me know if you hear anything," he called out to the group.

"Don't forget you have a meeting tomorrow in Augusta," Babs reminded. "Your accountant needs your signature on some documents he says he doesn't trust to send them electronically, even with Josh's super-secret methods."

"Damn, that hurts," Josh joked.

Nodding, he sighed. He did not mind the drive, but hated being around the hustle and bustle of workers in the early morning city traffic.

3

"Mom, I don't feel so good."

Sylvie Gardner squeezed the steering wheel tighter as she maneuvered through the early morning traffic around the school. Sparing a glance at her eight-year-old son, David, she tried to discern if he truly did not feel good or just dreaded his weekly spelling test. She reached her hand over and gently felt his forehead, noting he felt cool to the touch. Continuing to slide her hand up through his hair, she bounced her gaze between the road and David.

"Sweetie, I think you're just nervous today. We've studied those words and you know them backward and forward."

"It's my stomach," he explained. "It feels really yucky."

"I was worried about letting you go to that birthday party yesterday evening. I'm sure you ate way too much."

David nodded but kept his eyes forward, helping as usual. "Looks like there's a parking space up there, Mom," he said, pointing to the curb near the school.

She smiled and, with only getting honked at once, was able to slide into the tight space. Twisting her body so that she could face him, she longed to reach over and brush his hair off his forehead, but remembered the last time she did that when his friends were around he had given a little jerk. Eight years old. *He's growing up so fast.* Looking at her son's blue eyes and dark brown hair, that curled in the back, she recognized herself in his features.

"I hope you have a good day today," she said. He lunged across the console and threw his arms around her neck giving a squeeze. She hugged him back, surprised, but always glad for the show of emotions from her little boy. She never knew from one minute to the next, if she would be presented with a little boy or a young man.

She watched as he opened the door and hopped out of the car, his backpack straps perched on his shoulders. He turned and gave a little wave before walking over to meet with his friends. She knew her parking space was as valuable as gold, but could not help but sit for just another moment, watching as he disappeared into the school building.

Finally, pulling out into traffic before someone grew impatient, she glanced at the clock on the dashboard and recognized she needed to hurry to get to work on time. Their daily routine during the work week rarely changed and she looked forward to the weekends when they had more time to themselves. He still enjoyed trips to the zoo or just sitting and watching a ballgame with her on TV.

Once she made it to downtown, she continued to fight her way through traffic. Sitting at a red light she glanced into the mirror in her visor. Her dark brown hair was pulled back into a low ponytail. Her makeup was subtle, but at least it gave a little color to her otherwise tired face. The car behind her honked and she realized the light had turned green. *God, is this how my day is going to go? Please don't let David be sick today. Please let me be able to get to work on time. And please let Mr. Thomas not harass me!*

She made it to her building's parking garage and pulled into an empty space. With only a few minutes to spare, she toed off her flat shoes and slid on her heels. Twisting to the back seat, she grabbed her small briefcase and purse before jumping out of her car. Hurrying through the garage to the elevator, her eyes landed on an **Out of Order** sign taped to the front.

Huffing loudly, she glanced at her watch and trotted out of the garage, racing toward the front of her building as fast as her pencil skirt and heels would allow. Rounding the corner, she slammed into a wall, stumbling backward as a warm shower covered her front.

"Shit!" she cried, her arms flailing in an effort to keep from falling onto her ass as her purse and briefcase went flying to the sidewalk. A strong grip clamped about her arm, saving her at the last second.

"Fuck!" a deep male voice met her ears.

Righting herself, she looked up toward the voice, stunned at the sight in front of her. The wall was actually a huge man, tall and muscular. Wearing a buttoned shirt with the sleeves rolled up his thick forearms, she wondered how the buttons did not pop over his chest. His dark, black hair was short on the sides and longer on top, just enough to curl slightly. His square jaw was covered in a thick, five-o'clock shadow even though it was still morning. His full, lush lips were mesmerizing, but it was his eyes that captured her attention. So dark, the iris was indistinguishable from the pupil. And those eyes were staring at her chest.

Looking at the now-empty, squished, paper coffee cup in his hand, she glanced down as the warmth from her shirt penetrated her foggy brain. She realized she was now wearing his spilled coffee all over the front of her blouse.

"Oh, shit," she repeated, her eyes wide in horror at her ruined outfit. "I've got to get to work!"

Before she had a chance to curse further, he bent and grabbed her purse and briefcase with one hand while still holding her arm with the other. Quickly turning, he pulled her toward a dark SUV.

"Miss, I'm so sorry," he apologized, as he continued down the sidewalk.

Tugging against his hold, she opened her mouth to scream, when he spoke again.

"This is my vehicle...I've got a spare shirt I can give to you."

Her protest died on her lips as he let go of her arm and clicked the key fob, opening the back of the SUV.

Mace dug around in the ever-present bag he kept for possible night travel and came up with a slightly wrinkled white shirt. He turned to the still-stunned woman and held it out in his hand. She stood motionless, in shock, her eyes still on his face. He dropped his gaze to her chest where the tan stain covering her light blue blouse stood out in stark relief. The previously almost-full cup of coffee now covered her from chin to waist. Lifting his gaze again, he noted her rich, brown hair was falling out of her low ponytail, the loose tendrils blowing about her head.

She was much smaller than he, not surprising since he was six feet, five inches, but her curves were evident in her pencil skirt and stained blouse. Her large, blue eyes stared up at him, her beautiful face capturing his attention. Something about her tickled the recesses of his memory. He was sure he had seen her before...not recently...but somewhere, sometime.

He realized she was still staring at the proffered shirt and admitted, "I know it'll be large on you, but I assure you it's clean. Maybe if you...uh...tuck it in your skirt and...uh...add a sweater..."

Almost laughing at the ludicrous thought of wearing the huge shirt, Sylvie glanced back down and observed her own shirt completely covered in coffee. Unable to think of another course of action, besides calling the day a complete disaster and going home, she accepted his offering.

"Uh...thanks." She reached out and took the shirt, not having an alternative plan. He was so tall, she had to lean her head back to stare into his eyes. "How will I return it?"

"No worries," he hastened to say, clearly not wanting her to feel indebted.

"Right," she nodded. Twisting her head to look up at her building, she realized she had to hurry. "Uh…I have to…uh…go. Bye…uh, thank you," she babbled. Turning, she hustled toward the front doors, her face still aflame with a blush.

Mace stood, rooted to the sidewalk, watching the woman hurry away until she disappeared through the massive, glass front doors. The back view of her was good as the front and he realized, too late, that if he had given her his name, he could have met her again when she returned the shirt. *Not that I give a rat's ass about the shirt…but, I'd love to see her again.*

Entering the building, Sylvie hastened to the ladies' room, stopping to look into the mirror. The full view of her coffee-stained front solidified the need to change into the stranger's proffered shirt. Quickly stripping off her blouse, she was glad for the flesh-colored bra she was wearing, considering it was the same color as the coffee and therefore not showing more stain. Pulling his large shirt on, she saw it hung halfway down her thighs and dwarfed her torso. Standing for a moment, she dropped her chin to her chest in defeat.

Sucking in a deep breath, she let it out slowly before lifting her gaze, continuing. Rolling up the sleeves so they did not hang way below her fingers, she buttoned the front. Giving a quick tuck, she zipped her skirt before rolling and shoving her soiled blouse into her briefcase. With a last glance into the mirror, she hurried to the elevator.

Stepping out onto the fifth floor of her building, her heels tapped out a rapid staccato down the hall as she hurried to her desk. Her official title was Administrative Manager, but the men in the office treated her more like a secretary of days gone by. She not only did the tasks assigned to her, but also spent her time fetching coffee and occasionally going out to pick up their dry-cleaning. However, without having completed her Business degree, and as a single mom, she needed to work and the job offered decent pay and good benefits.

Walking into her small office, she grabbed the sweater hanging on the back of her door that she kept in her office in case she got cold. Looking at herself, she had to admit, she made the large, white men's shirt work. Knowing the tucked tails hung almost down to the skirt's hem, a grin slipped from her lips. Pulling on the cardigan, she smoothed her hands over her front, convinced no one would notice.

Her mind slid back to the man who offered his shirt for her. As upset as she had been, she realized what a chivalrous act it had been. He was tall...and dark...and undoubtedly handsome. Blowing out another breath, she could not remember the last time she had been in the presence of such a viral man...the kind of man whose masculinity poured from every cell of his being.

She moved to her desk and once more breathed a

sigh of relief that she had an office with a window. She did not mind if it was a cold, cloudy, rainy day or if the sun was beaming down warmly, she just loved being able to see outside.

Her view was not as expansive as it used to be, considering a new, tall building was being constructed across the street. She had to admit it was fascinating to watch the process. The foundation, the steel framing, and the construction workers starting at the bottom, building their way upward. Her building was only six floors tall, but the building across the street was going to be ten stories. The first six floors of the building appeared to be almost complete, with windows and workers on the inside of what looked to be offices, similar to hers.

While the street between them was very wide, she knew that one day she would be able to look out of her window and see other people at work over there.

"I swear, you should get some plants in here the way you love having your blinds up all the time," Jeannie said.

She turned from the window, a smile on her face as she greeted one of the few other women who worked in the office. "I might love the window and the natural light that comes through, but I'm horrible with indoor plants. I do not have a green thumb unless they are outside."

Jeannie walked into her office and plopped down in the chair. "How is it that we're only at the beginning of our day and I already feel like I'm ready to go home?"

Chuckling, she shook her head as she sat down

behind her desk, opening her laptop. "I don't know, but I hear you. Some days should just be over before they even get started."

Before they had a chance to continue chatting, a knock on the door frame had her lifting her eyes. She kept the friendly smile on her face, but it was forced. "Good morning, Matthew. What can I do for you?"

Tall, dark-haired, and dressed in an impeccable suit, he sauntered into the office and walked up behind Jeannie. Leaning forward, he placed his hands on her shoulders, giving her a little squeeze. "You feel a little tense here. Sure you don't need a massage?"

Jeannie jumped from her chair quickly, moving out of his reach. "No thanks, I don't think so. But, if I did, I wouldn't be getting one from you." She turned on her heels and walked out of the office after shooting a sympathetic look toward Sylvie.

Undeterred, Matthew turned his hundred-watt smile toward Sylvie, and said, "What about you, gorgeous?"

"Uh...no." Looking down at her computer, she tried to think of a polite and professional way to get him out of her office. Just then, another man knocked on the door, and called out, "Come on Matthew, we've got a meeting to get to." He looked at her, and added, "Don't forget the meeting we have at ten, and another one at three-thirty. Make sure you bring the files with you."

Matthew turned and walked slowly out of her office, winking at her as he left. Rolling her eyes, she grimaced. *When have I ever forgotten a meeting or the files necessary for it? And Matthew makes me cringe! Ugh!*

His mannerisms could be construed by some as sexual harassment, but he was careful to not ever go overboard with his actions. Just enough to make her uncomfortable, but not enough that she felt like she could fight successfully with Human Resources. *I need this job.* Sighing heavily, she turned back to her laptop, ready to start the day.

Hours later, after the first meeting was successfully completed and she was planning on eating her yogurt for lunch in her office while still working, her phone rang. Glancing down, she saw that it was the elementary school number.

"Hello? This is Ms. Gardner, is everything alright?"

"Hello, Ms. Gardner. This is the nurse at South Cove Elementary and I have David here with me. I'm afraid he threw up right after lunch and has a low-grade temperature. I need you to come pick him up from school."

Rubbing her forehead, she looked at the time on her laptop. If she left now, she would just be able to make it to the school and back during her lunch break, and make it for the afternoon meeting. Feeling guilty that her son was sick, she battled the feeling of being overwhelmed. Giving her head a shake to dislodge the thoughts of self-pity, she replied, "Yes, of course, I'll be there just as soon as I can. Thank you."

Shutting her laptop, she grabbed her purse, phone, and keys. Walking out the door, she hurried down the hall and ran into her boss. "Mr. Thomas, I'm taking my lunch out of the building and will be back in time for the afternoon meeting."

Even though he was the same height as she, he always managed to look down his nose at her. "Ms. Gardner, I had hoped we could go over some of the notes for the meeting during your lunchtime."

If I had a dime for every time someone wanted me to work through my lunch... "I'm very sorry, Mr. Thomas, but I have to go pick up my son from school. He's not well."

Pinching his lips together he heaved an over-exaggerated sigh, saying, "I wish I had known that you were a single mom when you were hired."

Anger flooded her veins, as she carefully said, "That line of questioning would have been illegal, as I'm sure you know. I've worked very hard for this company, and have made sure that my responsibilities as a parent have not interfered with the workplace. I'm taking my lunch, just like many people in this office who leave the building for lunch. I will be ready for the afternoon meeting. Now, please excuse me."

Her voice shook with rage, but she forced herself to maintain a professional demeanor. With a slight nod of her head, she walked past him, her heels clicking on the tile floor as she hurried toward the elevator.

Once in her car, she sucked in a shuddering breath, blowing it out slowly in an effort to calm herself before she began driving. Glancing at the time, she backed out of the parking space knowing she needed to hurry to keep her promise to the school, as well as to her boss.

"But Mom, I hate sitting in your office. It's boring. There's nothing to do."

Wishing she could count to ten to ease the stress, she knew she did not even have time to do that. Unable to believe all her backup babysitters were unavailable, she sighed. "David, honey, I don't know what to tell you. I'm doing the best I can. Mrs. Marshall is not at home today. Our neighbor, Mr. Curtis, is also not at home today and the afterschool care, that you are able to go to sometimes, does not take sick children. I've got no choice, please understand that."

Weaving quickly through the midday traffic, she pulled into her building's parking garage once again, sliding into a parking space. Glancing toward the now-working elevators, she saw Matthew, and several of the other men, coming back from lunch. Angry, once more, that she had been expected to work through her lunch hour when the men seemed to have carte blanche to leave whenever they wanted, made her tension headache pound even worse.

Looking to the side, she saw David's pale face and mother's guilt hit her. His fever was low-grade, just enough to make him feel irritable, but not really sick.

"David, I swear if I could do this differently, I would. But I have a meeting in a few minutes that I have to be at. If you'll just stay in my office, eat your crackers and sip on ginger ale, you can play on your iPad."

He nodded and she was grateful that he was such a good kid. While he had a typical boy's enthusiasm, he had rarely argued against her requests. They hustled to the elevator, thrilled that it was now working, and quickly took the lift to her floor. Walking down the hall to her office, she watched as Jeannie looked up and gave David a big smile and wave before cocking her head at Sylvie. Shrugging, she communicated silently with her friend that she had no choice but to bring him. Jeannie mouthed, *Good luck*.

Leading David into her office, she closed the door hoping for a few minutes of privacy. Hanging her coat on the back of the door, she then took his, hanging it there as well.

"Wow! Mom! Look how big that building is!"

She could not help but grin at the excitement in his voice, but cautioned, "David, shhh. Keep your voice down."

He twisted his head around and nodded, his smile wide. "Sorry, Mom. It's just been a long time since I've been in your office and can't believe how big that building is now. Look at all the workers over there."

She walked over to where he stood at the window and placed her hands on his shoulders. His eyes wide in wonder and interest, she was grateful he would have something to watch while she was at her meeting. "I know," she agreed, giving his shoulder a squeeze. "I was just looking at it this morning. I've loved watching this building being built. At first, it was the workers as they constructed the outside and now I've been fascinated as they've completed the insides floor by floor."

A knock on her door interrupted her thoughts and before she had a chance to ask them to enter, her door was thrown open. Matthew and Mr. Thomas stood there, their eyes dropping from her down to David. She caught an eye roll from Matthew and Mr. Thomas' face grew red.

"What—"

"My son had to leave school as he was ill this morning. He'll stay here in my office while we have the meeting."

"This is hardly managerial protocol," Mr. Thomas began. "I don't like the idea of him being here."

"I did not have any other alternative and he'll be fine here. He's a good boy, and will entertain himself in my office without disturbing anyone for the time it takes me to complete the meeting."

"Fine, but he," Mr. Thomas said, nodding toward David, "had better behave himself." Turning sharply, he walked out of the room, Matthew following.

Her shoulders slumping, she placed a hand on her stomach, trying to quell the uneasiness. The feeling that the men in the office would rather not have her in the position was obvious. If it were not for the pay and the benefits, she would tell them what they could do with this job…*and it wouldn't be pleasant.*

Kneeling in an ass to heels squat in front of David, she held his gaze, and said, "Okay, David. I need you to be very quiet and very good. Jeannie is right outside, if you need her, but please don't bother her unless it's an emergency. I promise I'll be back as soon as my meeting is over, but it might last for a little while. I've set the ginger ale and crackers on my desk and the iPad is there as well. You can play on the iPad, do your homework, or you can even sit and enjoy watching the workers across the street. I haven't seen any of them in the offices directly across from us, but if you sit closer to the window and look up you can see where they're still working on the floors above."

He gave her a hug, saying, "I didn't like those men, Mom. I think they're rude. But I promise I'll be good.

His understanding of her situation, despite his youth, warmed her heart. Hugging him back, she replied, "Thanks, sweetheart." With a kiss to the top of his head, she grabbed the files and her laptop off of her desk and headed to the door, shutting it quietly behind her. Walking down the hall toward the conference room, she felt sure that he would be fine.

Hours later, she doubted her sanity. The meeting had dragged on incessantly and she had already slipped out of the room twice for a supposed bathroom break, only to run to her office to check on David. By now he looked tired, bored, and irritable.

"Baby, I'm so sorry. I promise it will be finished soon." Looking out the window, she could see why he was bored. The building across the street was emptying of construction workers and she knew some of the people in her office that worked earlier hours, had left as well. Giving him a kiss and a promise to be back soon, she hurried back to the conference room.

He'll be fine, she tried to convince herself. *What harm can come to him from staring at an empty, construction building, across the street?*

4

The sun had passed beyond the buildings across the street, casting his mom's office in shadows. David had played with the iPad, finished his homework, and was now busy twirling himself in his mom's office chair. He knew with a queasy stomach, he probably should not try to get dizzy, but could not help himself. He twirled as fast as he could one way and then, using his legs to kick on the floor, twirled himself in the other direction.

He had peeked through her door and observed the large open office area was mostly quiet. Heaving a sigh, he stopped the twirling chair, allowing his head to stop swimming. Sitting at her desk he put his feet up on the windowsill, staring at the building across the street.

A movement caught his eye and he sat up straighter in the chair, his interest piqued. A man, wearing a hard hat, walked into the open office space directly across from his mom's. He was wearing a dark suit, which didn't really go with the hard hat, but what captured

David's attention was the bright red tie he wore. The man looked at his watch as he paced the room. He stopped and looked out the window and David dropped to the floor, ducking out of sight.

Peeking over the window sill, he saw the man continuing to pace. Climbing back into his mom's chair, he leaned forward again. The man reached into his pocket and pulled out a cell phone, bringing it to his ear. The man began talking, while continuing to walk around the room. He reminded David of his mom when she was frustrated and walking in circles.

So focused on the pacing man, he jumped when another man unexpectedly entered the room. He was also wearing a dark suit, but did not have a hard hat and his tie was blue. Without the hat on, he could see that his hair was gray. Before he had a chance to ponder why he wasn't wearing a hat, the two men began to talk, or rather, argue. It appeared they were shouting, their arms jerking wildly.

Eyes wide, he watched as the man with the blue tie turned and walk out of the room. Just as he got to the door, he turned around, and David observed the man's red face as he shouted something.

The first man pulled his phone out of his pocket again, but looked up as another man entered the room, this one wearing the clothes of the construction workers, including the bright yellow vest. The man with the red tie backed up a few steps, throwing his hands up, palms out in front of him. David's eyes grew wide. *This is better than TV!*

Turning, he picked up his mom's phone from the

desk. He had seen her use the camera app like binoculars when they were at the beach and she wanted to get a closer view of some seabirds. Holding the phone in front of him with the camera app turned on, he used his fingers to zoom in on the scene across the road.

The man in the suit had dark gray hair and glasses. The man he was arguing with had dark hair and was much larger, with a big, square head. Wondering when their argument was going to end, and getting a bit bored with it, he considered going to try and find his mom. She had promised she would be back soon after the last time she checked in on him.

The first man was looking down at his phone again when the other man stepped behind him, pulling something out of his pocket. His interest piqued again, David watched as the younger man made a swift movement with the rope in his hand, tossing it over the neck of the man in the suit.

Gasping, David jerked, almost dropping his mom's phone. Clamping his hands onto it, to keep it from falling, he continued to stare out the window, wondering if the two men were just playing.

The younger man jerked his hands back, tightening the rope, lifting the man in the suit off his feet as his hands clawed at his neck. They struggled for a moment, both falling backward, onto the floor. David jumped from his seat, but was unable to see them anymore. His heart pounded in his chest, but he did not know what to do.

Suddenly the younger man stood, his chest heaving the way David did after he had run for a long time on the playground. Finally, the man bent forward and David watched as he hefted the man in the suit, who was not moving, over his shoulder. He walked out of the room with the slumping man still over his shoulder, until they were out of sight.

David felt tears prick his eyes as he stood numbly, his body in shock. The last time he had spent the night with his best friend, they had watched a scary movie on TV that neither of their mothers knew they had watched. He had been scared but did not want to tell his friend they should not watch the movie. Now, he had an even worse sense of fear at what he had just witnessed.

Turning, he tossed his mom's phone on the desk as he bolted from the room. She was almost to the office, having left her meeting, and caught him as he flew into her arms. Dropping to her knees, she held his shaking body tightly, asking, "David, baby. What's wrong? What's wrong? Did you get sick again?"

He burrowed in, his arms clinging to her neck, and she rocked back on her heels, his weight almost taking them over. Catching herself, she stood and, as big as he was, held him tightly as she moved back into her office.

"David, what's wrong. Did you get scared?"

He nodded his head while it was still tucked beneath her chin. Sylvie's eyes quickly took in the room, seeing her phone and iPad on her desk, David's backpack casually on the floor and his coat still hanging on the back of the door. Nothing looked out of place.

Moving to her desk, she bent over and set him down on top. Cupping his face with her hands, she stared into his wide, terrified eyes. She could feel his body shaking underneath her hands and felt a punch of fear, straight to her heart.

"Baby, Mom's here. What happened, what happened?" She tried to keep her voice calm, but felt the words crack as they came out.

"O…over there. Mom, I saw the man over there."

"Over where, David? What man?" Her heart raced as she wondered if a man had entered her office and harmed her son. In the matter of a few seconds, her mind raced through the horrible possibilities and she cursed herself for leaving him alone, even though she was just down the hall.

He lifted a shaking hand and pointed behind him, not looking at the window. She jerked her eyes above his head, looking through the window, seeing nothing but the building across the street.

"What man? A man over there?"

His chin quivering, he nodded.

"So, there wasn't a man in here with you? You saw someone across the street?"

He nodded again and her breath left her lungs in a whoosh. Relief that he had not been assaulted in her office rushed over her and she had to force her legs to straighten or she would have fallen to the floor. Sucking in a deep, shuddering breath, she looked over his head again, seeing nothing across the street. *What had he seen? What could a man have been doing over there?* Her mind immediately jumped to the possibility of one of the workers urinating thinking no one was observing him, but she knew that, at his age, David would have found that amusing. Then she wondered if perhaps two workers had been fooling around, which would have confused him.

Sucking in another deep breath and letting it out slowly, she leaned down and felt him still shaking. "Okay sweetheart, you saw something happen across the street. I need you to tell me exactly what you saw. Go ahead and tell me everything and then I'll help you understand whatever it was."

His voice barely above a whisper, he said, "I saw him hurt the man. He hurt the man, Mommy."

He had not called her *Mommy* for the past couple of years, always using *Mom*. Hearing him revert, she stared at him wide-eyed, as she repeated, "Hurt the man?" At his shaky nod, she said, "Honey, I need you to talk to me. I need you to tell me exactly what you saw."

"A man came in, right over there. He was walking around and then talking on his phone. But then another man came in and it looked like they were yelling at each other. Then he left and another man came in."

He swallowed deeply and she gathered him in her arms as she moved to sit in one of the chairs in her office, cradling him. "Okay, that's good, sweetie. Keep going, tell me what else happened." Her brain, still jumping ahead, wondered if the two men had been arguing and that had frightened him. *Please, let that be all there is!*

He wrapped his arms around her neck, burrowing tightly, and said, "The man who came in last walked behind the other man. I didn't know what he was doing at first, but he threw something around the other man's neck and hurt him."

Her heart threatened to beat out of her chest at the idea of the two men across the way in a physical fight that her son had witnessed. "Okay, and that scared you? Did they leave?"

He shook his head as he pulled back slightly to stare up into her face. Whispering again, he said, "They fell into the floor, and I couldn't see, but the first man was kicking and struggling and trying to grab his neck. Then the second man got up and he picked up the first man and threw him across his shoulder. The first man wasn't moving, Mom. He just hung there. And then the second man carried him out, and I couldn't see anymore."

Her mind grappled to understand what he was telling her and whether or not he could have misinterpreted what he saw. While only eight years old, he had never been the type of child to exaggerate, and from his terrified eyes, pale complexion, and shakiness, she knew he was not lying.

She shifted him around in her lap so that she could stare directly into his eyes. "David, I need you to listen to me very carefully. Can you do that for me?" He held her gaze and nodded, a serious expression on his face.

"I'm going to ask you some questions and I need you to answer them honestly. Remember, you're not going to be in trouble at all for how you answer them, as long as you're honest. I know that you were in here for a long time. Did you perhaps fall asleep, and have a bad dream?"

He shook his head, and replied, "No, I didn't fall asleep."

"Okay, when you looked across the street, into the building over there, did you see two men talking and you imagined that they were fighting?"

His chin quivered and he shook his head again. "Mommy, I'm telling the truth. They were fighting and when the one man, who was bigger, picked the other man up, he wasn't moving."

"Okay, David, I believe you. But, honey, we can't go home yet. I have to call the police and report that you saw something. They'll send a policeman here who'll ask you questions and then they can go over there and see if they can find anything."

She was not sure if the idea of having to talk to a policeman was going to frighten him. But he solemnly nodded his head, and said, "You always said that the police help people. I want that man to get help, Mommy."

At that moment, if she ever had any doubts about his story, she knew he was telling the truth. Whatever he saw…whatever those men had been doing…he was telling the truth. And that realization terrified her.

Two hours later, Sylvie was still sitting in her office with David sitting next to her, his small hand clasped in hers. The police had come and questioned David over and over. It did not take much for her to figure out they were trying to trip him up.

They had sent two officers to the building across the street, and she watched from her window as they entered the room. David positively identified that that was the room where he had seen the men. The officers searched around but did not find anything on the floor. Another officer arrived and searched for fingerprints, but there were multiple ones, probably from all the construction workers.

David looked up, and said, "Mom, I didn't see them touch anything in the room."

She pinched her lips as she forced a smile directed at her son, before looking up at the officer in charge still in the room with them. Doubt in her son's story oozed from him.

"Detective Tragg, may I speak with you out in the hall for a moment?"

He nodded and stood as she kissed the top of David's head before leading the detective into the hall. Shutting the door behind her, she opened her mouth but before she could speak he jumped in.

"Ms. Gardner, I know your son thinks he saw something, but a young boy like that has an active imagination. I'm not saying he's wasted our time because we check out a lot of calls for things that never happened and I'll certainly have your report if anyone comes up missing. But, if you want to take my advice, take your son home."

"My son is not lying," she bit out, her insides quaking as she clasped her hands in front of her to keep them from shaking as well.

"Well, now, maybe that's true," he said. "But even you admitted he was running a fever today. Maybe in his fevered mind, he saw things that just weren't there."

Exasperated, she said, "He's not delirious. He barely had a fever. I don't know what he saw but he saw something."

"I understand that, ma'am, and you did the right thing by calling the police. We've taken the report. We checked out the scene. If anything else comes from this and we need you, we'll let you know."

Realizing that she was not going to get anywhere with the officer, she nodded and walked back into her office. Plastering a smile on her face for her son again, she said, "Come on, David. We can go home now. The police will take care of everything."

He looked up at her, and asked, "Will they get the bad man, Mom?"

She felt, rather than saw, Detective Tragg behind her. Keeping her voice steady, she replied, "Yes, David. I'm sure the police will do their job and try to find the man you saw."

She helped David put his jacket on, grabbed his backpack, shoved her phone and iPad into her purse and slung both over her shoulder. Taking him by the hand, she turned and, on unsteady legs, walked out of her office.

They had barely made it to the elevator when Mr. Thomas walked out of his office, his face red with anger.

"I can't believe you have the police in this building!"

Exhausted, she looked up at her boss, and asked, "Just what would you have me do? My son witnessed a crime and you want me to ignore it?"

Mr. Thomas leaned forward, growling, "This would

not have happened if your son had not been here, where he should not have been!"

"Oh, really? The crime happened because my son was here? The crime was actually witnessed because my son was here. So now, the police have a chance to find out what happened!"

Mr. Thomas leaned back, his fury barely in check. "I don't want your son here again. If you cannot handle your responsibilities for this job and combine it with your *motherhood*, then you may need to find another job."

Now, shaking as much from anger as from fatigue, she said, "Then I may just have to report your threat to Human Resources." The elevator doors opened and with David's hand firmly in hers, she walked in, jabbing the button to go down to the garage.

Looking up at her, his eyes teary, David said, "Mom, I'm sorry your boss is yelling and it's my fault."

Kneeling, she hugged him tightly. "Honey, I'm so proud of you. You were scared, but you did the right thing." Standing as the elevator doors opened, they walked to their car. "Let's go home. We could both use something to eat, and a good night's sleep."

As they drove home, she wondered if either of them would be able to sleep peacefully. Hours later, as David lay in her bed tightly snuggled into her embrace, she let out a long breath. Exhausted to her bones, she was afraid to close her eyes. Kissing the top of his head, she kept vigil all night.

5

Mace, Drew, and Rank stood near the opening of one of the caves as the sun set from behind them. It was a habit Mace had formed from the first night he owned the lighthouse. Every evening possible, he either climbed to the top of the lighthouse, stood at the opening of the large cave, or occasionally sat in one of the chairs at the back of the house. But he always tried, when not on a mission, to watch the sunset sky.

The others had left at the end of their shifts, the day providing new leads for missions and the completion of others. As night descended, the three of them walked back inside, securing the compound. Once they were upstairs, Drew and Rank said their goodbyes. Marge handed each of them a large slice of apple pie, wrapped in foil, saying, "Take 'em home, boys. I know you'll enjoy them."

As Mace took the supper plate she had prepared

over to the table, she spent an extra minute wiping down an already clean counter.

Looking over at her, he shook his head. "I know you've got something to say. When you start cleaning things that are already clean, I know you're just trying to figure out how to bring up something that I probably don't want to hear."

Huffing, she tossed the sponge to the sink and turned to face him, leaning her hip against the counter. "All right. Every one of those men is dedicated to this job, but they don't mind going out in the evenings or weekends when they're not on a mission. Go to a bar, hang with friends, drink, dance, even find a convenient girl for the night—" His eyebrows rose at that last one and she said, "What? You forget I was a young woman in the sex, drugs, rock n' roll sixties? My social life was a helluva lot wilder than yours! What I'd like to know, is what you have against having a little fun?"

Undeterred in taking a bite of the chicken casserole she had prepared, he chewed slowly, fighting a grin, before swallowing. Knowing she was itching for a response, he dragged it out as long as he could.

"Oh, good grief, Mace. No one takes that long to chew! You're just avoiding the question."

Chuckling, he wiped his mouth, looking at her with affection. "You know, if I didn't know what a badass you were, I'd almost mistake you for a mother hen."

Narrowing her eyes, she said, "I got all night if it takes that long for you to answer the question."

"I could just fire you, you know, for insubordination."

"Oh, hell, nobody's ever been able to get rid of me when I didn't want to leave. You don't scare me."

He agreed, nodding. "You're right, I doubt anyone could get rid of you. You're indispensable." He watched as she crossed her arms over her ample chest, her hip still leaning against the counter. Throwing his hands up in defeat, he said, "I honestly don't have a good reason. I've never been one to hit the bars to blow off steam and, other than an occasional pickup, I just haven't been that interested. On top of that, I'm sure as hell not interested in a relationship."

"And just why not? You've spent your entire adult life working for the defense of our country, at the expense of your own social life. You've now spent the last several years building this company, literally from below the ground up. I just hate to see you devote everything to your work, and not leave any room to take care of your heart."

Shaking his head, he replied, "Gotta admit, what you and Horace have is pretty cool to watch. But from what I saw from my parents, relationships aren't that easy and when they go south, they can go really bad."

"Sounds to me like you're just scared."

"Damn, woman. Those're fightin' words."

Grabbing the dishtowel from the counter, she tossed it at his head, but he threw his hand up, catching it deftly. Walking around the counter, she grabbed her purse and coat. "Well, you may have won this battle," she quipped, "but I'm in for the long haul. One of these days, I hope to see you settled like me and Horace."

With that she headed out the door, to meet Horace at their car.

He watched her leave and his smile slowly faded from his face. He was not opposed to having a relationship…a *good* relationship…he just had no idea how to go about it. An image of the beautiful woman from this morning ran through his mind and a chuckle slipped from his lips. Hair falling from the low ponytail, her subtle makeup playing up her features, her perfect curves, and her chest covered in his coffee. Shaking his head, he thought, *If I keep making first impressions like that, I'll never have a relationship!*

Sylvie lay awake, listening to David's slow, even breaths, as he finally slept. Terrified of being alone, he had quickly crawled into her bed. With the radio playing soft music and the night light casting a gentle illumination about the room, she finally coaxed his exhausted body to sleep.

Her thoughts swirled until she thought she would go mad. Mr. Thomas' irrational accusations and demands. The bad luck of not being able to find a babysitter that day. Her son being just slightly ill enough to not be in school. It was as though everything had conspired on that day to create a disaster.

As she had gotten changed for bed she had pulled off her forgotten, borrowed shirt and thought of the man who had given it to her. Rolling her eyes, she wondered what he must have thought of her. He was one of the most virile men she had ever met. Her ex-husband liked to think he was God's gift to women, but he had nothing on the tall, dark, handsome man whose shirt she now had. For a fleeting moment, she wondered if she had gotten his contact information whether she would have been able to see him again to return the shirt.

Groaning, she forced thoughts of him out of her mind, instead wondering about the scene her son had witnessed. *Were the two men actually fighting, or were they just roughhousing? Did a crime happen, or was it some kind of stupid joke that her unsuspecting son happened to see? Or, did he witness an assault? And, if so, what happened to the man who had been attacked?*

She could not say that Detective Tragg had been rude or overly dismissive, but as soon as his other officers reported that they did not see any evidence of a crime, it was clear he thought David either made it up or did not understand what he saw. *So, will they investigate further? Will they look for a missing man?*

As the minutes rolled by, and sleep did not come, she decided that neither she, nor David, would leave the house the next day. It would be Friday, and since he had been sent home sick, the teachers would not expect him to be there anyway. And, after the way Mr. Thomas had spoken to her, she needed an extra day to not have to look at his face.

Willing her mind to clear, she hoped that someone would care enough to see if a crime had been committed.

Unable to sleep, Mace went down to the compound and sat down at the computer. He liked the camaraderie and energy when his employees were here, but also liked the quiet solitude. Scanning through police reports, he set the parameters to the state level to begin with, planning on moving to national reports later.

With a practiced eye, he quickly read and dismissed most taglines until he came to one that caught his attention. *A boy reported seeing an assault in a building under construction.* If it had not been for the word *boy* he would have continued scrolling, but he stopped and read the entire report.

Office building. Man in suit. Man in construction vest. Both in hard hats. Size of men...description of men...cell phone...fight...rope around neck...larger man carrying out the first. For the boy to be eight years old, the details gave credence to his story. He scanned the report from the attending officers who searched the building but came up with nothing.

Shaking his head, he wondered what he was doing. LSI worked nationally and internationally on high profile cases...*and I make notes on a child's report of an assault?* But, he had a sixth sense about cases and this one sent his spidey senses tingling.

He hesitated, fingers over the keyboard, then clicked *save* and marked the file to look at the next day.

Staying awake for another half hour, he continued to search, saving a few more cases to keep an eye on, before going back up the elevator, and then climbing the stairs to his bedroom. His room, on the back of the house near the lighthouse tower, had a large window facing the water. It reminded him of his room at his grandfather's house, a mile up the road. He now owned that property as well, but only stayed there occasionally, preferring the nearness of the LSI compound. Staring out the window, the lights sparkling off the inky water, eased the tension he felt in the back of his neck.

His mind cast back to when he was a child looking out his window one night. There had been a boat moving close to the shore, and then two men on board dropped something heavy into the surf. When he woke his father to tell him, he yelled at him to get back to bed and stop bothering him. The next day, his father punished him for telling 'whoppers', but he knew what he had seen. He had recounted the tale to his grandfather, who immediately combed the shore to see if he could find anything.

Sighing heavily, he thought of the police report he had just read. *Since when do I let a childhood memory affect my job?* Climbing into bed, he pushed both the report and the past from his mind. Rolling over, sleep finally overtook him, but his dreams were a twisted mesh of childhood memories that slid into memories of his time in the Army...times he would rather forget.

It was only two o'clock in the afternoon, but Sylvie was dragging. Little sleep and large nerves had a tension headache blooming. She watched David carefully, afraid to leave him alone. It was obvious that he was anxious.

He ate little and was unusually quiet. No fever, no stomach ache, but his eyes darted around at every sound and she would catch him staring off into space, a heart-wrenching expression on his face as terror passed through his eyes.

Distracting him with ice cream, she was startled when he suddenly asked, "Do you think the police will get to the hurt man in time?"

Licking the dollop of ice cream off her bottom lip as she pondered how to answer, she finally said, slowly, "Well...I hope so. Uh...if he was hurt, then maybe the other man got help for him."

Her son's face registered doubt for a moment but he stayed quiet and continued to eat his ice cream.

She battled with what to say, her mother's mind for once coming up empty and with no one to turn to, she felt alone for the millionth time since becoming a mother. Before she had a chance to speak, he looked up, more doubt in his eyes.

"What if the man was dead?" he asked, his voice a whisper.

Deciding not to lie, she said, "I don't know, baby. I don't know."

Neither spoke as they finished eating. Standing at the kitchen sink, rinsing out the bowls, she watched as he went into the fenced-in backyard to play. He moved to the old swing set that was there when they moved into the house and quietly swung back and forth. Deciding she did not want to leave him alone with his thoughts for too long, she finished the dishes and moved to the door to join him.

Their house was on the corner and from her vantage point she could see a dark SUV parked down the street that she did not recognize. The neighborhood was an older one and they had little through traffic… and certainly not parked, tinted-windowed SUVs. Her hand rested on the door handle, unease creeping through her as she tried to convince herself she was being paranoid.

Unable to cease the fear slithering along her spine, she opened the door and called, "David, come in."

He turned his face toward her, his feet dragging on the ground to slow his swing. She watched as he opened his mouth to protest, but she jumped in, "I've got a surprise to show you."

Intrigued, he hopped from the swing and headed toward her. Her mind raced as to what surprise she could have for him. He stepped inside the house and peered up at her in expectation as she quickly shut the door.

"Uh…how about we go to a movie today?"

"On a school day, when I'm supposed to be home sick?"

Jesus, he's thinking more responsibly than I am! "Uh… yeah. I guess since yesterday was so hard on you, I think today needs to be special."

He nodded enthusiastically and she sent him off to get his jacket. Sagging against the doorframe, she glanced back out and with dismay saw the SUV still there. Refusing to look at it anymore, she hurried to check the movie lists as they headed out the door. *I hope there's a kid-friendly movie playing at the theater!*

Four hours later, they were back in the house and she was sitting on the sofa, shivering deep inside, while David was upstairs taking a bath. She had watched the black SUV follow at a distance when she drove to the theater at the mall. Once inside, she barely watched the movie as her eyes continually drifted to the door to see if some large, burly man with a gun had walked in. Even knowing her imagination was in overdrive, she could not stop.

Back in the car, she did not see anyone following and convinced herself that she had dreamed the entire sequence of events. David smiled often since leaving the theater and appeared more relaxed than earlier, which was a relief. With a deep breath out, she got up and headed into the kitchen to fix dinner, when she noticed the black SUV drive slowly down the street before it parked in the same place again.

No longer worried about what the police might think of her, she walked into the living room and grabbed her phone. Asking for Detective Tragg, she chewed her fingernail as she waited. He came on the line and she reported everything she had seen.

"Did you get the license tag number?"

"Oh…no, it was too far away."

"Can you see it now? Maybe take a picture with your phone?"

She hurried to the kitchen to look out the window over the sink, but the SUV was no longer parked there. "It's gone."

She heard the exasperation in his voice but he promised to add her call to his report. Disconnecting, she alternated between cursing her stupidity for not getting the license number and the police, for putting it all on her. Rubbing her aching head, she went around and double checked each window and door, making sure she and David were locked in tight for the night.

6

Mace looked up from the table as several more of his men walked in. Seeing Blake, he grinned his welcome before starting the briefing.

Blake, newly returned from a mission in California, reported, "I'll finish writing my notes up this afternoon—"

The others interrupted with chuckles at that pronouncement. They all hated paperwork, but Blake especially did. Flipping them off, he continued, "But, it all went like clockwork. I managed to get the Mexican Ambassador's daughter off the vessel she was on. The passengers all looked like a bunch of goddamn reprobates, but she kept swearing they were friends."

"You think she'll stay out of trouble?" Drew asked, slurping down his hot coffee, fresh from the pot.

Blake grimaced and said, "I'd like to think that since the boat was overtaken by pirates, a few of which were killed before the Mexican police showed up and whoever was still alive is now sitting in a Mexican jail, woulda shaken her up." Lifting his heavy shoulders, he said, "I talked to her, but who the fuck knows."

Mace nodded, saying, "We got her out of a dangerous situation that she put herself in. I'll let the Ambassador know he needs to bring her to heel, or we might not be able to save her next time she gets a wild hair." Looking back down at his tablet, he asked, "Cobb?"

Rank, running his hand through his still damp hair, said, "Got a message this morning saying the security for the Senator's mansion is up and running. He wants to recheck some items this morning and will be in this afternoon."

"Problems?"

"Don't think so, but the Senator's got a couple of kids and his wife is extra nervous and wants all precautions taken. It seems the Senator's far-reaching politics has certain extremist groups upset."

Nodding, he asked, "How was the run?"

Rank grinned, saying, "Reminds me of SEAL training. I ran along the coast then decided to do a little swim in the ocean."

"Little?"

"Ah hell, just a few miles," Rank replied, puffing out his chest in mock self-admiration.

A few balled-up pieces of paper were thrown and he tried to bat them as they came, succeeding only part of the time.

"Tate, get your report to Babs before she has a coronary. We're almost at the end of the month and she's got to get the invoices out."

Tate nodded, but grimaced, as he held up his hands. "I got hands that can fire a weapon, eyesight that can spot a mission from a further distance than most people, but trying to type out a goddamn report makes my teeth hurt."

"If you just dictate your notes in a way that I can understand what the fuck you're talking about, I'll type them up," Babs yelled from across the room.

Tate's eyes opened wide, mischief clear in them, until Mace said, "Don't even think about it. Or at least not until I can hire someone else we can trust to work on reports. Babs is overworked as it is, just doing everything else I got her doing. So, get your reports in. Everybody."

He looked down, scrolling through the tablet to see what else was coming up. Just as he was getting ready to end the meeting, sending everyone to their assignments, Rank spoke up.

"You got a note here from last night about some police chatter. Anything I need to look into?"

He rubbed his hand over his jaw. "Nah, just something that caught my eye. Nothing major...it sort of stuck with me. I decided to mark it for future notification and thought I'd work on it today."

Nodding, Rank said, "Okay, no problem. I just saw another notification has come in for that one. I'll let you check it out."

He acknowledged the information and after a few more minutes discussing assignments, everyone was dismissed to go about their day's work. Immediately moving to his computer, he looked up the new notification. There was not much in it, as it looked like the detective in charge was in a rush. *So, the mother of the child who thought he saw an assault, reports that a strange vehicle was parked outside their house and had followed them.* His brow crinkled in concern. *The detective didn't think this was a reason to check things out?*

Shaking his head, he knew the situation probably did not warrant LSI's involvement, but he could not get the report out of his mind.

"David! Let's go!"

"Mom, where are my cleats?"

"In my hands."

Sylvie stood at the bottom of the steps, David's cleats dangling from one hand, her purse in the other as she checked her keys and cell phone. David came flying down the stairs, his baseball uniform on, his eyes bright with excitement. She hadn't seen that look in several days and was glad to see it back on his face.

"Help me out, sweetie. Grab the snack bag off the kitchen counter."

Before he had a chance to move, her phone rang. She looked down, and said, "Oh, it's Julie." Answering the phone, she snapped her fingers to get David's attention, and mouthed, *Get your extra cleats out of the mudroom.* A moment later, she disconnected just as David came running back in. "Thanks. Calvin was already on his way to practice when his mom realized he didn't have his cleats and she can't get there right now. I assume it's okay if he wears your extra pair?"

"Sure!" he enthused, running toward the front door. "Let's go!"

Once at the ballfield, David ran off to find his friends and teammates and she settled into the camp chair that she brought, sitting next to the other parents. For the next two hours, she tried to forget her worries and everything that happened over the past several days. Focusing on cheering for the children and David's smile, she felt better.

As the game ended and he ran over to her, she suggested, "How about hamburgers?"

He jumped up and down and she smiled at his enthusiasm. *Kids recuperate so much faster than adults!*

An hour later she and David pulled into their driveway. She glanced over at her son and could not help but smile. He seemed less traumatized than the previous days and, with no sight of the mysterious, dark SUV, she hoped their nightmare was over.

"Put your cleats in your room, honey," she said, as they climbed out of the car and walked to the front door.

"Sure Mom."

Stepping into the entry foyer of their small home, she immediately threw her hand out to the side to keep him from barreling into the house. Her eyes wide, she looked around in suspicion. Nothing was overtly out of place, but she instinctively knew that someone had been in the house. The pictures hung at slight angles on the wall. Her magazines that had been spread out across the coffee table, were now stacked. "David, take my hand."

"Mom, what is it?"

"I just want to check through the house a little bit," she replied, hoping he did not hear the quaking in her voice. "I'd like you with me."

They moved together into the kitchen, where she had the same feeling. To anyone else, the room looked normal. To her, she knew someone had been there. Making David stay in the kitchen, with promises of cookies, she hurried upstairs, finding the same thing. Noticing the clothes in her closet pushed to one side, she clutched her stomach, the sight of her things having been touched by an intruder cutting into her.

Hurrying back downstairs, she grabbed her phone and stepped out onto the front porch. Calling Detective Tragg, she winced as she heard herself describe what she had found. *He didn't believe me before... why do I think he's going to believe me now?*

Within thirty minutes, he and another officer drove up. She gave the two of them a tour of the house, explaining every change she noticed. Though she could see the doubt in their eyes, the officers went through and fingerprinted most of the items that she said had been touched. Taking her fingerprints as well, to cross-match, they promised to look into it.

On the way out the door, Detective Tragg turned, and said, "I know you think I don't believe you but, I promise I'm treating this just like any other investigation. I want you and your son safe. You might want to check into getting deadbolts for your doors, because what you have here would not keep anyone out."

She nodded, numb and cold to her bones, simply thanking him before shutting the door after he left. Flipping the flimsy lock, she turned around and faced her son. The renewed look of fear on his face gutted her once more.

7

Mace met with Walker as soon as he returned to the compound, taking notes on his recently finished mission. From all accounts, it sounded as though everything had been completed satisfactorily and he sent the finalized report to Babs.

"Sounds good, man," he said. "Make sure you get your travel vouchers to Babs, as well."

"Thanks boss. What's up next for me?"

"I don't want to send you back out on another flight right away. If you and Cobb want to drive to the capital, we've got some more security work lined up."

He watched as Walker gave a chin lift in response before walking over to his computer and settling in. Turning back to his desk to scroll through reports, he was curious to see if there was anything else on the child who'd seen the assault.

Finding another notification, he quickly clicked on the link. Reading through the new report of the home invasion, he could no longer ignore his gut. Shaking his head, he became frustrated with the detective on the case, who clearly had little imagination. Everyone at LSI knew that things rarely fit into neat little boxes when investigating.

Beginning to slide through the possibilities, grateful the media had not gotten hold of the story, he began to analyze. One theory was whoever had been in the other office, had looked over and seen the child watching them. If the child was there with a parent, it would not be difficult to find out whose office that was. If indeed there had been an assault, then it would be in their best interest to find and silence the child.

Another possibility, one that made him even more nervous, was that someone dirty in the police force had seen the report and was suppressing the investigation. Leaning back in his chair, he tapped his fingers on the desk, trying to decide what to do. If that person had truly intruded into the home of the witness, then they were escalating.

So far, there had been no mention of a father. Clicking on Sylvie Gardner, he jolted as her driver's license photograph appeared. *The woman I spilled coffee on!* Suddenly he realized where he had seen her before. *Ed Gardner's wife.* He remembered seeing her occasionally at a few of the Army events, before he was accepted into the Special Forces. He had met Ed in boot camp and, like everyone who knew Ed, knew he was a royal fuck-up. So sure of his own abilities, the man had dragged the platoon down. Once out of boot camp, Ed had been certain that he would be selected for Special Forces, but never made the cut. *Never came fuckin' close.*

With a few more taps on the keyboard, he quickly discovered they were divorced. Court documents showed abandonment, no steady employment, no alimony payments, and no child support payments...*Once an asshole, always an asshole.* He clicked more and discovered she lived in a small house in an old neighborhood, probably with no security. Steady job. Son in elementary school. Checking out her social media, he was pleased to see that she posted little and only had one photo of her and her son.

That picture, much more flattering than her driver's license, showed a beautiful, dark-haired woman and a cute little boy that appeared to take more after his mother than father.

Before he had a chance to look at anything else, Babs called out. "Mace, the Governor is on the line. Highest priority."

Immediately picking up on their secure line, he said, "Governor Sanders. What can LSI do for you?"

"I like a man who can get down to business immediately. We've got a situation that the media will get hold of very soon. I'd like to have you handle as much as you can outside of the media circus that will be following the State Police." He hesitated, for only a second, before blurting, "Charles Jefferson, the new State Attorney, is missing."

"For how long, sir?"

"Since last Thursday. He left the office, told his assistant that he had some official business to attend to and would not be back into the office until the next day. His wife is out of town…actually, she's in Hawaii, for a real estate agents' conference. He did not report into work on Friday morning, nor did he call. His assistant tried calling his cell phone numerous times and finally got hold of his wife who had not heard from him. She flew back in yesterday and reported that it appears as though he has not been in the house for at least a few days."

"We can start investigating immediately but, with the State Police working the case, I'm assuming you want us to go through the back door."

"Yes. I've already informed Detective Martinez that you'll be working the case with him."

"I've worked with Roberto before. He's an excellent detective and won't get his nose out of joint if we work with him."

"Good, good. Charles is an asset, a good State Attorney. But, I've got to tell you, what he was starting to work on was going to bring some heat down on him."

"I had read in the news that he was going after organized hate groups…ones that had big money backing them."

There was a long sigh before the Governor said, "Yes. I tried to tell him that to start off with something so monumental was going to be difficult. But, he was elected on a platform of being hard on hate groups."

"We'll begin immediately, sir," he confirmed.

"Thank you. We'll be in touch."

He disconnected and called the Keepers together.

"Whatcha got, boss?" Blake asked.

"We have a new mission, priority one." He quickly explained his conversation with the Governor. "I'll take the lead and I'll need three or four others with me on this to begin with. Walker, Rank, Tate." He looked over at Babs taking notes, and said, "Everyone else, continue on with your assignments and we'll call you in as we need to."

As the group disbursed, the ones working with him moved over to the conference table. "I'll be with you guys in just a minute."

Heading over to Josh, he said, "I'd like you to do something for me, please." Typing in a few things on his tablet, he pulled up the police report that Sylvie Gardner had filed. "Can't explain this, other than I have a gut feeling. Would you just check into this and see if the police follow up?"

"You got it, boss. No worries."

Silently appreciating his dedication, no questions asked, he headed over to the main conference table where he and the others began the investigation into the missing State Attorney. Showing them the information the Governor had given to him, he added, "I want to know who Jefferson was looking into, see if we can follow a trail of where he went after he left work on Thursday."

Tate immediately moved to one of the computers, where he was able to follow the traffic cameras. Within thirty minutes, he called out, "It looks like he took his car from the state capital building, drove downtown and parked in one of the parking garages. There are cameras in the garages and I see him at 2:43 PM exiting his car. He goes out of camera range and does not come back. I can fast-forward the time and see that no one else has been in or around his car."

"Forward that on to Detective Martinez."

A couple of the men grinned, having worked with the lead detective before. "Thank God Roberto likes working with us."

"He'd be an idiot not to," Rank said. "We've got better toys in our sandbox."

Cutting in, he said, "Get into Charles' computer. I want to find out if he was trying to meet with anyone."

As the LSI team began working, Josh motioned to him with a head jerk. Walking over, he asked, "Whatcha got?"

"I set an alert on Sylvie Gardner and it appears she used her credit card to purchase several deadbolt locks."

He leaned over Josh's shoulder and checked out the transaction. Sighing, he said, "She bought some shitty-ass locks."

"You got a special interest in this? Something you want me to keep looking into?"

By now, several of the other men had turned their attention toward them. He stood up, rolled his shoulders back and stretched his neck, shaking his head slowly.

"Hard to explain. Couldn't sleep the other night so, I just started looking at some statewide police chatter. Came across a report where a young boy told his mom that he witnessed an assault in the building across from where he was hanging out. His mom believed him, absolutely. Police were more doubtful, but they checked into it. Didn't seem like it was anything."

"Not really the typical thing that LSI looks into, boss," Clay said. "Not that there's anything wrong with that. Just wondering, I suppose."

He looked around the room at each of the men, all the top of their fields. "Every one of us has developed a sixth sense for when something just doesn't feel right. I know that sense has saved my ass more than once. Probably yours, too." He watched the flashes of understanding move through the eyes of the men as they looked at him, most nodding.

"Something about the story struck a nerve with me. Granted, I'll be honest and say it reminded me of a time when I was a kid and my dad didn't believe something that I had seen. My grampa did, but it was too late to find out anything." Shrugging, he added, "Hell, maybe it's just me being sentimental. I've got no fucking clue but, it caught my eye so, I flagged it. Now two other reports have come in from the mom and I get the feeling that the police are going to shove this under the rug and file it under the *not to be believed* file."

Drew looked up, and volunteered, "Right now, I'm finishing up the last of my identity changes for a client. You want me to start looking into this?"

Mace hesitated and Drew stared at him carefully. "Or, maybe boss, you want to check into it yourself. Don't take offense but, if it's striking a personal chord with you, then maybe you should be the one to check it out."

He rubbed his chin, staring at his boots. The other

men watched him carefully, not used to seeing him struggle with an inner decision. He finally looked up and nodded slowly. "Got to admit, when I looked the mother up, I recognized her from my past. Her ex-husband was in the Army the same time I joined. An asshole who was dishonorably discharged about the time she divorced his ass for abandonment. The Governor's request takes precedence over everything, but yeah, I'm going to take a look into this."

"Where did this happen?"

"Downtown Augusta…near the capitol. She lives on this side of the city."

Tate offered, "You could go today. We're all going to be finishing our missions or starting the intel on the missing State Attorney. Nothing much you could do here anyway."

"Boss, I've got the address sent to your phone and you should be there in less than an hour," Babs piped up, her sharp eyes on him.

Shaking his head at the high-handedness of his crew, he met their eyes. "Then I guess I'll see you later today or tomorrow morning." With goodbyes and good lucks called out, he headed to the elevator.

8

Walking toward the house, Mace noticed there were no outdoor security lights. The front of the small house held a porch, allowing easy access for someone to look in or break into the front windows. Approaching the front door, he spied an old lock, but no security deadbolt. Sighing, he pressed the doorbell, then stepped back several feet.

"I'll get it!" a child's voice could be heard.

"No! Wait on me!" a woman's strident voice called out.

He was glad to hear that she was going to stop the child from opening the door, but was unprepared for the wide, blue eyes that peered up at him when the door swung open. He remembered them from the other day, but had been so distracted by their collision that he had not appreciated them fully.

Sylvie kept one hand on the doorknob and with her other hand, held David back. Glad that she had locked the screen door, she looked up in surprise at the large man standing on her porch. Dark, black hair. Heavy five o'clock shadow. Khaki cargo pants that did little to hide his thick thighs. And a tight, black T-shirt, that did nothing to hide his muscular torso. *The man from our coffee disaster!*

"You? What are you doing here?"

Mace reached into his back pocket, pulling out his identification. He held it open and leaned forward just enough for her to be able to read it. "I'm Mason Hanover. I was wondering if we could talk."

Sylvie's eyes jumped between the ID badge held in front of her and Mason's face. She felt David lean around her hip, but kept her hand firmly on his shoulder.

"Oh, cool! Are you like a special agent?" David asked.

Mace's eyes moved from Sylvie's face down to the boy at her side, seeing excitement written on his features. "I'm a private investigator," he said, before looking back to her.

"I'm afraid I don't understand," she said. "Is this about your shirt?"

"No, no. I'm here in conjunction with the police reports." She bit her lip, indecision written on her face and he was momentarily distracted by the sight of her plump lips. Forcing his eyes to stay on hers, he said, "I know of the trouble you've been having," he gently nodded toward David. "I'd like to help, if I can."

"I'm sorry, I still don't understand. Did someone send you?"

Lifting his hands to the side, he said, "You're right to

be suspicious. I'll tell you what...how about if I sit out here on the porch and we can talk through the screen door. This way your son can play safely inside, you'll still be behind your locked screen door, and I'll be out here in plain sight."

"Wouldn't that seem rather odd?"

"I suppose—"

"Sylvie! Is that man bothering you?"

He glanced to the side and saw an elderly, snowy-haired man standing by the fence, a rake held high in his hands. He stepped back away from the door, allowing the neighbor to see him clearly.

"No, Mr. Curtis," Sylvie called out through the screen door, watching as Mason stepped down from the porch and walked toward the fence. Curious, she leaned as close as she could, with her nose smushed against the screen, hoping to hear what was being said.

Mace approached the man, stopping about ten feet away, his hands clearly visible. "I'm glad to see Ms. Gardner has a neighbor so watchful. I'd like to show you my ID if you don't mind."

The older man pulled his head back, narrowing his eyes. "What kind of ID?"

"My name is Mason Hanover and I'm a private investigator." He pulled out his ID, held it in his hand and walked toward Mr. Curtis, who scrutinized it carefully.

"What do you want with Ms. Sylvie? She doesn't need any trouble."

"I absolutely agree and that's why I'm here. I'd like to help look into who might be bothering her. I'm gonna sit on the outside of her door with her screen locked, and she and I are going to chat. I feel better knowing that she's got a neighbor keeping an eye on her."

Mr. Curtis nodded and looked past him, toward the house. "Looks okay to me, Ms. Sylvie. But I'm going to be here in the yard to keep an eye on things."

With a nod, Mace turned and walked back up to the house, pulling a porch chair next to the door. He noticed that Sylvie had moved a chair as well and was now sitting on the other side of the screen.

Looking down at David, she said, "I need you to go play, sweetie. You can either play in your room or watch TV in the den. I'm going to be sitting here at the door, having a chat with this man."

Scrunching his nose, David looked up at her. "You're going to talk to each other through the door?"

Before she had a chance to answer, he spoke up. "I want to make sure that your mom is comfortable talking to me. I'm a stranger to you guys right now. This way, I'll be in plain sight of the neighbors and she can be on the inside of a locked door."

David's lifted eyebrows continued to show surprise but, lured by the idea of watching any show he wanted on TV, he nodded and bounded down the hall.

Sylvie watched her son before turning around, observing as Mason settled into the chair.

"I'm going to be completely honest with you, Ms. Gardner," he said. "I am a private investigator, but I also do a lot of individual security work. I monitor police reports at times, to see if I can be of service. The police report that was filed last Thursday caught my eye."

Cocking her head to the side, she asked, "Did you recognize me from our little…um…encounter that morning?"

"No, no…not at first. Then, I saw your driver's license and realized who you were."

She nodded, uncertain what to say, but curiosity filling her.

"I felt a desire to look into the reports that you had filed with the police here."

"What is it that you're looking for?"

"After seeing the third report that you filed, where you reported someone had been in your house, I wanted to offer you any security advice that I can." Doubts still lingered in her eyes, so Mason continued, "For example, I see that you have no deadbolt on your front door and I assume the back door is the same. I also notice that you do not have any outdoor security lights. And, while Mr. Curtis is certainly the kind of neighbor who would call the police if he thought something was happening, I would hate for you to only have him to rely on."

"Mr. Hanover, everything you say is right, but I've talked to the police. I don't know what else I can do," she said, dropping her eyes, wiping her palms on her jeans. "I bought a deadbolt lock, but after I got home, I realized I need a special drill bit to make a large hole in the door to install it." Her voice lower, she admitted, "I can't afford any fancy security."

"Ms. Gardner, do you believe that your son witnessed a crime?"

Her head jerked up, her clear eyes meeting his, and

she declared, "Absolutely. He may be young, but he doesn't lie. And while he certainly has a child's normal imagination, the level of detail was too descriptive for him to be incorrect in what he saw." She glanced over her shoulder, presumably listening for the sound of the television, before she looked toward him again. "I'm the one that had to hold him that night because he was shaking in fright."

"I believe him," he said, noting her jerk in surprise at his words. "I know the police were doubtful, but I believe your son's story. What concerns me, is that you had somebody checking out this house, following you, and then you reported that someone had been inside. That indicates to me that what your son saw was absolutely real."

Sylvie's breath left her lungs in a rush, and she whispered, "Thank you." Closing her eyes, for just a moment, she reveled in how good it felt to have someone believe them. Focusing on him again, she said, "But, I don't know what to do about any of this."

"When I was checking the police reports, I didn't see a witness drawing. Did they ask him for specific details?"

Nodding, she said, "Yes. David gave a description of what the men looked like and were wearing, but…" As her voice trailed off, it struck her that the police had not asked for more details.

"I'd like to talk to David if you don't mind," Mason said, carefully watching the concern and doubt etched into the lines of her forehead. The idea that he would like to erase those lines by smoothing his fingers over her skin struck him, but he battled the idea back as soon as it hit. He expected her immediate refusal, but to his surprise, she nodded.

"Yes...okay."

"I could—"

"Please, come in," she said, standing quickly. Pushing her chair back, she reached forward and flipped the simple latch on the screen door. Seeing his surprise, she said, "I trust you. I want you to talk to David...as long as you don't scare him more than he's already been scared."

Pushing open the door, she leaned her head out and called to Mr. Curtis, still standing dutifully by the fence. "Thank you, Mr. Curtis, but Mr. Hanover will be coming in now."

"You sure?" the older man called out, lifting his cap from his head as he wiped his brow.

"Yes. You get inside where it's more comfortable. Thank you!"

The two of them watched him amble back toward his house, before Mace turned her way, saying, "He might not be much strength in a fight, but a good neighbor who keeps watch is a great security."

He observed her smile and was struck again with just how pretty she was. Once more, the desire to keep the smile on her face and worry lines away moved through him. Blowing out his breath, he stepped into the house.

With a practiced eye, he took in the details in one sweep. Living room and dining room in the front. Hall leading to kitchen and den. It was small, but clean and neat. He wondered how she managed with a young boy, but before he had a chance to ponder that further, she turned and said, "I'll get some lemonade and then we can talk to David."

She moved to the kitchen and he walked into the living room. The mantle held family photographs but none, he noted, included Ed. It was as though he had been erased from their lives...*or maybe he did the erasing before he abandoned them.*

After a few minutes, she reentered the room with a tray containing two glasses of lemonade and one of milk, a boy right behind her. He jumped up and took it from her hands, setting it on the coffee table.

Blinking, Sylvie was surprised at the gentlemanly behavior. With her hand on David's shoulder, she introduced him. David looked up in anticipation, but remained quiet.

Sitting down, she prompted Mason to talk to David to explain why he was there.

David stared, his eyes bright.

"You want me to describe the men?"

"Yes, please. I need to you just walk me through what they looked like...in detail. But, make sure to stick to just what you saw. Let's start with the first man."

Taking a big drink of milk, David nodded solemnly. "He had gray hair, but not like Mr. Curtis."

"How was it different?"

"Mr. Curtis' hair is real thick and all white. This man's hair was cut short and was gray and kind of thin on top." David turned his face to her and said, "Like grampa's hair."

With a benevolent smile, she lifted her eyes back to Mason. "My father is almost bald on top but he still keeps a few longer hairs to try to make it look like it's there."

He grinned and with a nod to David, encouraged him to continue. "And his clothes?"

"He was wearing a suit. It was dark and he had a bright red tie. I remember thinking that Grampa would never wear a tie like that."

"Anything else? Like, was he tall or short? Skinny or heavy?"

David's brow knit in concentration before he replied, "I don't know how tall, but he wasn't heavy. He was about the same size as the other man in a suit, but shorter than the man who hurt him."

After having David describe the second man in a suit, he nodded and asked, "Okay, what can you tell me about the third man?"

"He was kind of fat—uh, sorry, Mom." He glanced at her before looking back at Mason. "Mom doesn't like me to say that word."

"It's okay right now, sweetie," she said, thinking that her son could use any descriptive word he knew, even if it was not nice.

"Okay, so he was taller and heavier?" Mason confirmed.

David nodded enthusiastically and added, "He wore a blue shirt and blue jeans and one of those orange vests that the construction men wear." Sitting up straighter, he added, "Oh yeah...also a yellow hard hat like the man in the suit was wearing."

"Sounds like you had a really good view of them," Mace noted, opting for a casual line of questioning. Still, he observed Sylvie's posture stiffening. Ignoring her, he kept his gaze on David.

Once more, David nodded. "It was easy to see them at first but then I got more curious. So, I tried to see them closer."

Sylvie, who had recognized Mason's subtle questioning of David's account, had all objections fly out of her head at her son's words. Swinging her head around, she gasped. "What? What do you mean you tried to see them closer?" She heard the rise of hysteria in her voice, but surprise and fear took over.

Doubt moved over David's face as he slumped down in his chair. "I'm sorry, Mom. I used your phone. I wanted to zoom on them."

Mace jerked his gaze to Sylvie, whose face registered shock. She looked at him, as well, giving her head a little shake. He opened his mouth to ask her to get her phone but she had already jumped up from her seat.

Sylvie ran to the kitchen where her phone lay on the counter. As she turned to head back, she slammed into Mason's large body. She would have fallen if it were not for his hands, which darted out to clamp onto her upper arms.

Barely aware he was holding her, she clasped the phone in her hand as her eyes held his. "Here. Here it is."

"But, Mom," David called, hurrying into the room. "I just used the zoom on your camera. I wasn't trying to take their picture."

Staring into Mason's eyes, her voice barely a squeak,

she said, "My phone's old and the keys are kind of wonky. I take pictures all the time without meaning to."

He looked down at the older model phone clutched in her hand, her knuckles white. Calmly, he said, "Let me see it, please."

She nodded but, frozen in place, did not move, so Mace gently removed it from her fingers. With a few taps, he brought up her photos. There...the last ones... were shots David had taken when he was trying to look through the zoom lens.

His eyes widened, not believing what he was seeing. The photos were slightly fuzzy, but he knew LSI had the equipment to discern the details. With a few more taps, he sent the pictures to his email.

Looking at the dark circles underneath Sylvie's wide, blue eyes and the strain lines on either side of her mouth, he forced a smile on his face and gently said to David, "I think that's good for now. You wanna go play while I talk to your mom?"

9

The two of them watched David bound down the hall, then, Sylvie turned to Mason. Her voice a raspy whisper, she asked, "Did he...are there...pictures?"

He nodded, but held on to her phone, not showing the evidence to her. "Yes. I'm sending them to my company who can work to identify the men he saw—"

"I had no idea he used my phone! I would have turned it over to the police—"

"I'm glad you didn't," he interrupted. Seeing her brows lower, he said, "Right now, I'm not convinced that someone isn't checking to see what reports you've made with the police."

"Someone?"

Shaking his head, he said, "Someone who's keeping track for the wrong reasons. And, if that person, or persons, knew this was on your phone, you could be in danger."

Her knees buckled and he snatched her by her arms

again, barely keeping her from hitting the floor. He assisted her to a chair and watched as she lifted her hands to cover her face.

Mace watched as Sylvie's body hitched, realizing she was silently crying. Moving swiftly, he knelt by her chair, bringing his face close to hers, and took her hands, holding them in his own. "What can I do?"

She swallowed, gulping air, and cried, "I almost didn't believe him. Even when I was swearing to the police that he would never make it up, there was a part of me that wondered if it could have possibly happened." She raised her head to peer at him. "What does that say about me?"

"I'd say it makes you perfectly normal," he replied, gaining a confused look from her. "No, really. Most kids his age blur truth with what they see on TV or hear from others at school. I'd be doubtful also."

"It's just his level of detail was so complicated for an eight-year-old child. I couldn't imagine that he was making it up, even when my mind didn't want to accept it. I don't let him watch scary things on TV, so I couldn't imagine where his story could have come from if it hadn't happened right in front of him." She pulled one of her hands free from his and swiped at her tears. Inhaling deeply, she let her breath out slowly. "I need to go check on him. I can get us more lemonade."

It was on the tip of his tongue to say *no*, thinking he should get back and begin running the photographs through his computers. Plus, the idea of spending more time in the presence of the beautiful Sylvie, was not the best plan. But instead, his mouth opened, and he replied, "Yeah, I'd like that."

Suddenly, David ran in from the den, peering up at him as he addressed Sylvie. "Hey Mom, can Mr. Hanover play catch with me? I need some help and you're really not very good."

"David, I'm sure Mr. Hanover has—"

"That'd be great. I haven't played catch in a long time." He followed David toward the back door, passing a visibly stunned Sylvie. With his lips curving into a smile, he headed out to the backyard.

It only took a few minutes for him to realize that David definitely needed some pointers. Working with the young boy, he found he was a very quick learner.

David grinned widely when he caught the baseball in his glove, and said, "You're a really good coach, Mr. Hanover. Mom tries, but she throws the ball all over the place. I have a hard enough time catching it when it's thrown straight."

Mace laughed, and said, "I'm sure she's trying her best."

David's smile left and was replaced with a solemn expression. "Mom does try…she really does. A lot of my friends have moms *and* dads, so I know it's hard on her."

His heart jolted at the wisdom of David's words. Placing his large hand on his shoulder, he said, "I'm sure there's nothing more important in the world to her than you. And that makes being your mom easy."

The smile slowly returned to David's face as the two of them continued to practice catch.

Inside, with the fresh lemonade made, Sylvie picked

up the tray and walked to the door. Staring at the scene in front of her, she watched her son's look of concentration as he threw the ball and his huge grin when he caught it in return. Sighing, she knew that there were certain things she was not good at and wished his father had wanted to have a role in his life.

Ed had desired a pretty wife to be at his side, always telling her that it would be important when he was a big deal in the Army. Those days never happened and she felt the brunt of his anger every day. After she had David, he made it evident that he did not want to have a child until his big dreams happened, so she left, divorcing him, without asking for alimony or child support. All she wanted was the freedom to raise David away from a mentally and emotionally abusive father. It had been a while since Ed had come around asking for money, threatening to make her and David's lives hell if he did not get it. Sighing heavily, she gave herself a shake, forcing those thoughts from her mind. Squaring her shoulders, she walked outside.

Noticing Sylvie coming through the back door, her hands full, Mace immediately stopped and took the tray from her, setting it on the small table. David came over and the three of them sat, sipping the lemonade in the shade. Always wary, his eyes moved around, noting the unsecure backyard and the street to the side, where he knew the vehicle had been parked. There was a fence surrounding the yard, but it was only three feet tall, leaving the backyard completely exposed.

"What happens next?" she asked.

Casting his gaze toward David, he said, "I'll take the

pictures back to my office and use my... um... computers to see if I can get a better idea of who we're looking at." Standing, he picked up the tray, and said, "Let's go back inside."

As they moved through the back door, David darted into the den, plopping himself in front of the TV. Sylvie rolled her eyes and looked up at him, saying, "I normally don't let him watch TV so much."

"Don't worry on my account. I'm glad he has the distraction so we can talk a little bit more." Seeing her brow furrow, he moved in front of her, placing his hands on her shoulders. "I believed David's story but, obviously now that we've seen the pictures, we have proof. I want to make sure you're safe. Would you consider going to a safer location, until—"

"He's got school," she protested, her face contorting in indecision. "I don't know what to do. I want to be safe, but..." She sighed heavily.

"Look," he said, his hands squeezing gently on her shoulders. "Your safety is the most important thing and I want to see to that."

Sylvie tried to ignore the feel of Mason's strong hands on her, but the slight pressure gave comfort. Closing her eyes for a moment, she longed to give her cares over to him. "What do I do?"

Normally decisive, Mace hesitated, seeing her face. "You have virtually no security here. Do you have a friend you can stay with for the night? I can get my men over tomorrow to set up a system."

"Um...no, not really. I can't think of anyone and, even if I did, I wouldn't want to put them at risk."

With his hands still on her shoulders, he could feel the tension radiating through her body. "We're already into late spring. When does he get out of school?"

"He has two more weeks, though, the state assessments finished last week. But, this is the time that the kids look forward to so much, with field days and a chance to enjoy school without so much pressure."

Nodding slowly, he made a decision. It wasn't easy, given he was battling a surprisingly possessive desire to grab her and David and haul them off to safety. "I, or one of my men, will stay on guard outside at night until we get your security up or we find who is after you."

Biting her lip, she said, "I hate for you to go to that trouble, but I would be foolish to turn down the offer of help."

"Good." Before letting her go, he added, "I've got to go into my office and take a look at these pictures. I'll be back just as soon as I can and will stay the first night outside." Her eyes widened as they jumped to his and he added, "And please, call me Mace."

Her lips curved slightly and she nodded. "All right. And, well, I'm just Sylvie."

"Okay." Smiling toward the den, he called out, "David, you stay inside with your mom and, tomorrow, I'll take you to school and then after school, I'll show you some cool things I will have added to your house to make it super safe."

David grinned and said goodbye as Sylvie stood with her hands clasped in front of her. "This all seems so surreal," she admitted.

"I know," he agreed, "but tomorrow, when you get home from work, I'll have your house safe and secure."

She nodded and as he turned to leave, she reached out, placing her hand on his arm. "Mace?"

As he turned around, she hesitated before asking, "Why are you doing this?"

He hesitated, as well, before placing his hand over hers, "Let's just say, you remind me of someone. Someone I wasn't able to rescue a long time ago."

Leaving it at that, he turned and walked back to his SUV, carefully scanning the area as he went.

"Hey, Mace," Josh called out, sitting at his computer. "I'm just getting the photos from Ms. Gardner's phone cleaned up."

Mace walked over to stare at the screen. He had reported in to the others when he got back and, while they had listened to everything with interest, they were particularly intrigued that David had taken pictures, even accidentally.

Leaning over, he watched as Josh worked his magic and brought the pictures up on the large screen, making it clearer with each tap on the keyboard. Staring, his heart dropped in amazement.

"Holy shit."

The others in the room quickly turned, looking up at the screen, several mirroring his response. There, clearly identifiable, was the missing State Attorney. First, arguing with another man, whose face was never toward the camera, and then, slung over another man's shoulder...either unconscious or dead.

Mace raced along the road, cutting the time it took to get back to Sylvie's almost in half. Unable to reach her by phone, he had quickly given commands to his team and jumped into his SUV. They had forwarded the pictures to Detective Martinez along with Mace's report from talking to David, including the possibility that someone from the local police had been leaking the details.

Punching the numbers again, he listened as her phone rang, but no one picked up. *Where the fuck can she be?* The possible answer to that question made his blood run cold.

Taking a curve a little too fast, he forced all thoughts from his mind other than getting to Sylvie and David. The little boy, whose face had peered up at him so innocently, desperate for some male attention, reminded him so much of himself. *I never got it much from my dad, but thank God for Grampa.*

Sylvie moved to the front of his mind. When he first recognized her, he remembered her as a shy, quiet, young woman. Beautiful but, being married, he gave her no more than a passing thought. In fact, to be honest, he mostly felt sorry for her just for being married to such a dick.

Then, slamming into her the other day, spilling his coffee all over her blouse, he had been struck with her beauty. Assuming she would be horrified at his offer of a shirt, he had been impressed when she had accepted it.

She had grown into an even more beautiful woman and her strength of character shown through. Maybe it was because she was a mom. Maybe it was because she found the strength to kick Ed to the curb. Maybe it was just life's maturity. Whatever it was, she had something that drew him in.

Dialing again, his breath left him in a whoosh, surprised to hear David answer the phone.

"Hello? Mr. Hanover?"

"Where are you? Why hasn't your mom been answering her phone?" he asked, forcing his voice not to growl.

"Mom was at the fence, talking to Mr. Curtis. I heard her phone vibrate, but I'm not supposed to answer it."

"Is she still over there?"

"No, she came in and is taking a shower. I kept hearing her phone vibrate, so I decided to see who it was. She gets upset if it's…well…um… I saw it was your name, so I thought it would be okay if I answered."

The idea of her in the shower slammed into him, but with a quick shake of his head to refocus, he said, "I'm on my way back. You stay inside the house and I'll be there in a few minutes."

Coming into town, he slowed just enough to not draw the attention of the police, glad that her house was close. Knowing his men were not far behind, he jerked into the driveway.

Fighting the desire to run and break down the door, he slowed his breathing, forcing his mind to carefully analyze what he was seeing. A few neighbors were out mowing their grass, while some children played basketball in one of the driveways. There was no evidence of a strange vehicle in sight. Her car was parked in the same place as when he left earlier in the day.

Fuckin' hell, she didn't even have her fuckin' phone with her. What the hell would she do if someone was trying to get to her?

He quickly notified his team that he was at her house and told them he would meet them later. As he climbed from his truck and stalked toward the front, the door opened and there she stood. Hair sleeked away from her face, still damp from the shower. Dressed in comfortable yoga pants and a blue T-shirt, she looked delectable.

Tilting her head to the side, Sylvie watched Mace's powerful body move toward her. "David said you called—"

He placed his hand on her stomach and gently pushed her backward, till he could kick the door closed with his booted foot. Seeing David lurking behind, he leaned in close, and said, "You gotta keep your phone with you."

She looked up at his granite jaw, wondering what was happening. "I was right here. I didn't go anywhere," she responded, her words coming out in a breathy rush.

"I've been trying to call you for an hour."

Focusing on the tone of his voice, her eyes widened, and she asked, "What's wrong? Something's wrong?"

Deciding to keep her in the dark, for now, about the identity of the man David saw, Mace said, "I just wanted to get back so that I could start my shift. From now on, I want someone on you at all times." He inwardly cringed at the double meaning of his words, the idea of him on her, in bed, flashing through his mind. *What the fuck is wrong with me? I've never felt so blown over by any woman before.*

Sylvie felt the heat of blush rise up her face as Mace's words settled in. Knowing he was talking about security, she felt foolish for having thought, even for a second, about him on her for a completely different reason. Blowing out her breath, she nodded quickly and forced a smile to her lips. She may have gone a long time without sex, but she refused to let this man know how desperately he affected her.

10

Wanting to deny the attraction he felt, Mace searched for reasons to not talk to her, but Sylvie had insisted he stay for dinner and it would have seemed rude to refuse since she had fixed food for him. But, with dinner, lively conversation, and discovering what a well-mannered and intelligent child David was, he had to admit that he was comfortable…as long as he forced his mind off her delectable lips.

He had informed her that as soon as one of his men came to watch her house, he was going to have to leave to take care of some work, but would be back as soon as he could.

Sitting in his SUV, on the street, he noted the quiet night of the neighborhood. The neighbors all turned in early, the children's balls and bikes left abandoned in their yards, and everyone safely ensconced in their houses.

Headlights came down the street and he recognized

Tate's truck. As he pulled alongside him, they both rolled down their windows.

"The others are ready for you," Tate informed him. "They'll meet you there."

With a nod toward the house, he said, "All's quiet. I'll be back as soon as I can."

"You don't have to hurry on my account, boss. I'm good."

"I know, but I told David that I'd take him to school tomorrow. I don't want to break my word." If Tate thought there was any other meaning to his words, he did not let on. Driving away, he watched the house become smaller in his rearview mirror, strangely looking forward to when he would be back.

Twenty minutes later, he pulled his vehicle onto a narrow street, parking behind a dark van. Moving swiftly, he entered it, seeing Bray, Rank, and Drew already inside.

"Bray, welcome back. You up to speed on this one?"

"Thanks, boss. Absolutely. I reviewed the details on my flight back. Babs has my report from my last mission as well."

"Good man," he nodded and finished getting ready. Quickly donning dark pants and zipping up a dark hoodie jacket, he buckled on his equipment belt. "Report."

"Ms. Gardner's office building is two blocks away and the building in question is on the other side of the street. We clocked seven men keeping an eye on the perimeter."

Lifting his eyebrow, he silently questioned.

"Not professional. Haven't identified any of them yet, but they may be construction workers or rent-a-cops paid to keep an eye on the building now. Or, could be mob soldiers. One way or another, we'll have no problems."

"Clay shutting them down?" Clay often stayed in the compound, altering the traffic and building security cameras, generally making sure they could get in and out of a place without detection.

"He says we are a 'go'."

Slipping out of the van into the darkness, they moved to the building behind Sylvie's office. With no trouble, they made their way inside, heading to the basement. Jogging through old city tunnels, they moved beyond her building and into the basement of the construction site across the street.

Using night vision goggles, they easily found the staircase and quickly ascended to the fifth floor. Moving down the hall, they ascertained that there was no security inside the building. Mace hung back, allowing Rank to take the lead.

Entering the room that would have been across from Sylvie's office, they carefully searched. "David said that Charles was standing in the room, pacing and talking on his cell phone."

"Who do you think the other suited man was that David saw? And was that planned?" Bray asked, theorizing out loud.

"If they struggled, I wonder what happened to his cell phone," Rank commented, kneeling on the floor, his light sweeping over the area. Shaking his head, he added, "This room has been swept clean."

Mace moved to the room next to it and found it covered in sawdust and footprints. Moving back to the others, he said, "Someone cleaned this room, making sure to get rid of any evidence of a struggle."

"What about the police who came here to look? Either they were rookies, stupid, or dirty," Drew shook his head.

Making sure the room was just as they found it, they slipped back down the stairs, to the basement and through the tunnels to where they exited the building.

"You going to be at Ms. Gardner's tomorrow for the security?" Rank asked.

"Yeah. I'm taking David to school and making sure she's settled. Once we get the security up and I'm sure she's safe, then I'll be back in."

Within the hour, he was back in front of Sylvie's house, watching as Tate drove down the street. Shifting in his seat, he found a more comfortable position. He chuckled, thinking about the many nights when he was in the Special Forces, sleeping on the ground with a rock for a pillow. His SUV was infinitely more comfortable than those days.

He cast his gaze toward the house, seeing a single light in an upstairs window. It was late, but it appeared Sylvie was not sleeping. A few minutes later, he noted another light in the downstairs come on.

Inside the house, Sylvie found sleep was elusive. Unable to keep from peeking outside, she noticed when a truck replaced Mace's SUV. Tossing and turning provided no rest and the next time she looked out, hours later, she saw that Mace had returned.

Restless, she thought about the man who had invaded her home and her thoughts. At first, he appeared cold and hard. Almost scary, in fact. But, after having watched him play ball and gently coach David, he did not seem frightening. Over dinner he had relaxed and she caught him smiling more than once.

Ever since David was born, she had taken on the independent role of single mom. Sighing, as she rolled over once more, she realized how exhausting that was. She discovered how nice it was to have someone else help make a major decision with her. *Ed never did that.* As always, when her thoughts drifted to her ex-husband, she wondered about the young, idealistic—*hell, naïve*—woman she had been when she met the former soldier.

Grimacing, as she always did when she thought of him, she flopped onto her back, refusing to give him time in her mind. Looking at her clock, she accepted that sleep was not coming. Rising from bed, she pulled on her robe and walked down the stairs, belting it about her waist.

Pulling back the living room curtains, she pressed her face against the window, peering into the darkness. She wondered if Mace was sleeping but, then again, if he were on duty, he would not be. Walking to the door, she threw it open and stepped onto the front porch.

Mace watched as the front door opened and Sylvie stepped out. Standing underneath the porch light, her long hair fell about her shoulders. The blue flannel robe, loosely belted at her waist, did little to keep his mind off the curves that lay beneath.

Surprised to see her, he quickly alighted from his SUV and stalked up the front walk. Stopping at the bottom of the stairs, he looked up, seeing dark circles underneath her eyes in stark contrast to her pale complexion.

"Are you okay?" he asked. She nodded, without speaking, her eyes never leaving his. The air seemed to crackle between them. "Is something wrong?"

Emitting a small snort, she said wryly, "Now what on Earth could possibly be wrong?"

Unable to keep his lips from curving into a smile, he rested his hand on the railing. "Yeah. I see what you mean. But, knowing someone is outside your house, keeping an eye on everything, should make you rest easier."

"I know," she admitted, tucking her hair behind her ear. "The reality is, though, having the need for a security person to be outside my house is what keeps me awake." She stuffed her hands into the pockets of her robe and looked down at her feet for a moment. Lifting her chin, she held his gaze, and said, "I feel bad about you being in your car. Would you like to come in?"

Seeing him about to protest, she quickly added, "You'd be more comfortable on the sofa."

"I'm not sure that would be a good idea," he said, the battle between wanting to spend time with her and letting his guard down warring inside. "But, I wouldn't mind a cup of coffee."

Her smile beamed and she nodded. "Then at least come on in and keep me company while I fix it."

Walking up to the top of the steps, his gaze caressed her face before he whispered, "That, I can do."

Locking the door behind him, he followed her into the kitchen. She turned suddenly, jumping when she almost ran into his body. His arms shot out to catch her and she rocked back, looking up in surprise.

She blushed and said, "I keep running into you." His eyes bore deeply into hers and she looked down to avoid the intensity of his gaze. "Good grief, you're wearing boots and I still didn't even hear you behind me."

"Army training," he said, offering a simple explanation.

"You were in the Army?"

Nodding, he watched as she filled the coffee carafe with water before turning to look at him over her shoulder.

"When?"

"A few years back."

She spooned the coffee into the filter before switching it on. Turning to face him fully, she leaned back against the sink. Continuing her line of questioning, she asked, "Where were you stationed?"

"Quite a few places during my tours. I started out at

Fort Benning." He was not surprised when her eyebrows lifted.

"I was there. Actually, that's where David was born."

"And David's father?"

A look of disgust crossed her face as she crossed her arms in front of her. "He was in the Army," she admitted. "I'm afraid it didn't quite work out the way he hoped."

"Is he still in the Army?" he asked, wanting to see what she would say about him.

"Hardly. Ed had big plans, but had little ability to follow them through." Lifting her shoulders slightly, she added, "And, when his great plans fell apart, he tended to take his frustrations out on me."

Stunned at the revelation he had not anticipated, he felt anger coursing through his veins. There had been no record of domestic violence, which meant she never reported it.

Sylvie turned back toward the counter and, reaching up, pulled down two mugs. Unaware of the rage building on the other side of the room, she walked to the refrigerator, taking out the creamer.

"He took his frustration out on you?"

Mace's voice, almost an octave lower than his already deep voice, caused her to turn and look at him. She sucked in a quick intake of breath, wondering what had compelled her to give out that detail. *It makes me sounds so weak. I hate that Ed still has the ability to make me feel weak.*

Shrugging once more, she said, "It's in the past. Things happened. I didn't like it. And I wasn't going to have it around my baby. So, I ended the marriage and he didn't seem to mind." Heaving a sigh, she added, "It's not that I thought ending a marriage was something to be taken lightly, but I could not allow his abuse to be focused on David."

Leaning forward, his clenched fists resting on the counter, Mace asked a question that he already knew the answer to, but wanted to hear what she had to say anyway. "Does he pay alimony? Child support?"

Her eyes jumped back to his, taking in his visible anger, but not understanding it. "I'm sorry, Mace. I don't think that's any of your business."

"Fair enough," he agreed, but did not like it. "But, can I ask, is he still involved in David's life?"

To avoid answering the question, Sylvie turned back to the counter, the coffee now ready. Pouring two mugs full of the rich brew, she asked over her shoulder, "Cream? Sugar?" When he didn't answer she turned her head to look at him. The hard set of his jaw was still evident and she got the feeling that he was not used to someone not answering him.

She pushed his mug forward on the counter toward him, before moving the cream and sugar closer as well. Fixing her coffee the way she liked, she leaned back against the counter and took a sip. "I can see that you're not happy with my silence," she said. "I'm afraid, Mace, that you'll find I'm not one to give in so easily."

Mace sucked in a deep breath through his nose before letting it out slowly. Admiring her fortitude, he reached for his coffee cup and sipped it black. "That's good coffee. I like it strong."

Her lips curved as she took another sip, "Thank you. That might have been the only thing that Ed ever complimented me on...my coffee."

They continued in silence, for a few more minutes, each to their own thoughts and sipping the hot brew.

Sylvie looked at Mace, and said, "I know I'll never get to sleep after drinking this, but it's comforting." Seeing him nod his agreement, she found herself uncharacteristically wanting to talk more. Nodding toward the kitchen table, she walked over and took a seat, pleased when he did the same.

"I'm not sure why, after all these years, I'm still prickly about my ex-husband. The truth of the matter is, I've always been embarrassed that I chose poorly. I had a happy childhood and remember my dad always telling me that I should wait for a prince. The problem was, at twenty-one, I had no clue what to really look for in a man. Ed was very charming when we dated, full of big promises of Army glory. He talked incessantly about joining the Special Forces and how it was going to be nice to have me on his arm at all the functions we would attend." Snorting, she continued, "I was young, naïve, impressionable, and fell for his dashing manner and confident words."

"What happened?" Mace watched her focusing on her coffee as her fingers tightened around the cup. Mentally bracing, he waited for her to reply.

"He made it through boot camp but became angry that he was unable to apply for the Special Forces right away, insisting that he was more than ready. I was unaware of how much he drank, but it was affecting his work and the security of what he needed to be doing. He would take his anger out on me, verbally, but not physically...at least not at first. I became pregnant and rejoiced in thinking that a child might make him satisfied. Instead, it just made him angrier. One day, shortly after David was born, he came home, had been doing grunt work all day long, and he was furious. He didn't like what I had fixed for supper and he slapped me across the face, calling me horrible names—"

"You've got to be shitting me?" Cold ice ran through his veins and he felt his fingers spasm, surprised the ceramic mug did not shatter under the pressure.

She lifted her eyes and held his gaze steadily. "I left that night. I was not going to stay with a man who hit me and I was not to have my child raised in that environment. I offered him an easy out—no alimony, no child support. I wanted nothing from him."

"And David? Does he know?"

"He was a baby during the divorce, so I'm the only parent he's known." Almost as an afterthought, she added, "I would have allowed Ed to be part of David's life if he wanted, even after what he'd done, because a boy should have a father. But if he'd treated David in any way like he'd treated me, I would have ended their relationship. In the end, none of that mattered, because he didn't want to be there."

Shrugging, her face pinched, she continued, "Of course, David's asked about his father. He knows most of the truth, but he's only a child and I'd never lay anything on him that he can't handle. I suppose it's a sad state of affairs when many of his friends have divorced parents, so he doesn't think too much about it."

Silence settled between them as they continued to sip their coffee. Sylvie surreptitiously glanced Mace's way, unable to decipher what he thought of her marital confessions. She almost admitted that Ed never asked to see David when he approached her for money, but that was an embarrassing fact she was not ready to reveal to anyone.

11

After taking David to school and making sure Sylvie got to work, Mace went back to her house to wait for his men to show up. Not sleeping the night before was not what had his stomach in knots. It was the revelation about her ex-husband. It was one thing to have remembered him as a jerk, but something else entirely to know that Ed had taken his hand to her.

He would have felt this way about any man and woman but, that it was her, seemed to have brought his blood to boil. Seeing his men arrive, he was grateful for the interruption.

As Walker got busy, he went over the plans with Rank. "We need outside lights, security for all doors and windows, and a tie in directly to the police and our monitoring." Satisfied that they had it well in hand, he climbed back into his SUV and drove to the lighthouse.

Anxious to see if they could determine what Charles had been looking for when David saw him, he hurried inside, sending a hasty greeting to Marge and Horace. Once downstairs, he settled at the table and asked, "What was he working on?"

"Digging into his work files," Bray said, pulling up his notes. "He's had investigators working on the money laundering of some of the hate groups in the state."

"Anyone in particular?"

"The National Supreme Endeavor Group."

He narrowed eyes as he tried to recall what he had heard about this particular group. "They sound familiar, but I can't say that I remember what their deal is."

Bray nodded toward Drew, who took over. "They tend to fly under the radar because terrorism isn't their thing. They're an antigovernment group that engages in groundless conspiracy theorizing or advocates extreme antigovernment doctrines, often warning others of the government coming into their homes and taking over their lives. They're moving in the direction of trying to influence elections and have been suspected of laundering their money for years to keep their tax-free status in place."

"How far had Charles gotten?"

"State Police had gathered evidence and when they presented it to the State Attorney, he agreed it was enough to take on. So, his office is now running the investigation and it looks like he was going to keep pushing until he could prosecute."

"Any idea of who they were running money through?"

Bray said, "I talked to Roberto just before you came in and he said that his office is now tasked with finding

Charles Jefferson, using the photos that Ms. Gardner's son took. They're looking into the group but, the money laundering case is taking a back seat to finding him...or his body."

"Right now, I haven't gone through all Charles' files, but I wondered why the fuck he was in that building after the workers went home," Josh commented.

Drew spoke up, "The construction company is Crossover Building Company. The owner is Doug Smiteson."

"Any ties to the National Supreme Endeavor Group?"

"Not overtly, but I'm still digging."

Blowing out his breath, he nodded. "Okay...so, right now, we've got a State Attorney who's still missing and a small boy who was the only witness to his disappearance. He was last seen at a building site owned by the Crossover Building Company, which may, or may not, have anything to do with the investigation."

"Think it was just a random location for him to meet someone?" Blake asked.

Mace rubbed his chin, his mind working over the notes in front of them. Shaking his head, he said, "No. The assailant came in a construction worker's vest and hard hat. Charles knew enough about where he was going to have a hard hat. And, David said that Charles was looking at his watch and talking on his phone. That would indicate he might be there to meet someone specific and called when they didn't show."

"And when the other man in a suit came in?"

"I don't know. He might have been the person

Charles was supposed to meet...or a replacement and that's why Charles was so angry. Maybe it was just someone to keep him busy until the assailant got there."

Babs looked up from her desk, her phone in her hand and called out, "Walker's calling in. Says they're finished at the Gardner house."

Nodding, he said, "Good. I'll head back over in a couple of hours to pick David up from school, swing by and get Sylvie, and then show them the system we have in place."

Looking at the group, he said, "Let's follow the money trail. Cobb, you're the financial expert. You take the lead and see what you can get."

Cobb nodded, asking, "You want me to follow Crossover Building or the extremist group NSEG?"

He thought for a moment and said, "Chances are the building company will be easier, so start with them. But, specifically look for any link with NSEG." Before anyone left the table, he added, "Just for the record, the State Police are the legal investigators and our position is to protect Sylvie and David. It's a weird coincidence that I had already decided to provide protection for them based on the police chatter but, now that they're officially involved in the Charles Jefferson investigation, it makes it easier."

"Easier?" Drew asked, his brows lowered.

"Easier for us to investigate in order to keep them safe. So, while Roberto takes the lead for Charles, I want to find out who the fuck is threatening Sylvie and David. All roads will lead to the same group I'm sure, but my focus is their protection."

The men agreed, but shared grins. Turning away he shook his head. There was no way to hide it. His normally stoic personality came alive when discussing the two Gardeners who were now in his life.

Sylvie waited outside her office building, having told her boss she was leaving early. She sighed heavily at the withering look he had bestowed upon her at that news. Balancing on the knife's edge of keeping her job, she wondered why she bothered at all. *Oh, yeah...it pays the bills.* Rubbing her forehead, she tried to shove all the dueling thoughts out of her mind. Looking up, she spied Mace's SUV moving closer and she smiled, tossing a little wave.

She tucked a wind-blown strand of hair from her face, then blushed. *God, I'm not a young girl interested in flirting with a handsome man...been there, done that.* But, in her heart, she knew he was everything Ed had not been.

His intense expression softened when he saw her and her stomach flip-flopped as a smile spread across his full lips. He pulled to the curb and she ran around the hood to get to the passenger side.

He leaned across her to make sure she was buckled and her breath caught in her throat at his nearness. As he settled back, placing his hands on the wheel again, she said, "I feel bad that you have to come to get me—"

"Don't," Mace interrupted. "I didn't want you to go into work today, but since you insisted, taking you and picking you up was the next best thing." His gaze focused on

Sylvie, seeing the nervousness in her eyes. Instinctively, he reached his hand over and placed it on hers, giving a little squeeze. Speaking gently, he asked, "How was work?"

She closed her eyes, but was unable to keep the grimace from crossing her face. Shaking her head sadly, she replied, "I don't know." As a rueful snort slipped from her lips, she added, "I don't know what I'm doing in a job that doesn't appreciate me. I don't know what I'm doing working for a boss that is demanding and demeaning, all at the same time. And, right now, I don't know what I'm doing about David—"

He heard her voice crack and watched as she turned her head away, blinking at the moisture that had gathered in her eyes. Unable to stop himself, he leaned forward and with his free hand cupped her cheek, turning her face toward him again. "Hey, try to put the job out of your mind. Right now, focus on you and David. I've gotta say, you're doing a great job as a mom."

"But…I'm scared…"

He gently caressed her cheek with his thumb, and said, "From what I've seen, you're a wonderful mother. And you're doing everything right…believing him and keeping him safe. He's lucky to have you. And, if you're scared, that just means you're smart."

"Smart?" Sylvie stared into Mace's masculine face, the concern in his eyes taking her breath away.

"Yeah, smart." A slow smile curved Mace's lips, the feel of Sylvie's petal soft skin underneath his hand drawing him in. He leaned closer, barely aware that she did the same, until their faces were a few inches apart.

A car horn sounded behind them, jerking him back to his senses. Unable to believe he had almost kissed her at a time when she was vulnerable, he dropped his hand and turned away, grabbing the steering wheel once more.

"Sorry," he mumbled, not wanting to see the censure in her eyes.

Cold seeped through Sylvie and she leaned back in her seat. She had been so focused on Mace's deep eyes and his thick, sensuous lips that she hoped were coming toward her, that she had forgotten where they were. Seeing his professionalism slip back into place, she could feel the heat of blush burning her skin. Refusing to trust her voice, she said nothing as he pulled into traffic.

Once home, Mace walked Sylvie, with David tagging along asking questions, through the new security on their house. Floodlights had been installed on the front, sides, and back. Set to motion, he showed them how they would work. All windows, on both floors, had been wired, as well as the front and back door. He instructed them on how to set the security and had them both practice the codes several times, until he was sure they knew them.

After a while, David ran off to play, and he and Sylvie stood in the front foyer. She dropped her eyes, fiddling with the hem of her shirt. He lifted his hand toward her, but halted, dropping his arm back to his side.

"Well, I guess I should go," he said. Even as the words fell from his mouth, he stood rooted to the floor.

Tired of playing it safe, Sylvie lifted her eyes and observed Mace's gaze was on her. Rushing the offer, she asked, "Can you stay for dinner? It's not fancy, but we'd love to have you."

For only a few seconds, Mace battled the desire to stay against the knowledge that he should leave. Finally giving in, he smiled and said, "Yeah. That'd be great."

Her relief was evident on her face, her smile widening. "Good. Good. I'll get it started."

David ran back to them, and asked, "Is Mr. Hanover staying for dinner? Can he play with me?"

Sylvie saw the eagerness in her son's face and her heart squeezed. *What am I doing? The last thing I want is for David to get used to somebody showing him attention, only to leave.* Before she could find a way to rescind the invitation, Mace spoke.

"Sure, bud. I'd love to."

She watched David's face morph from hope to utter joy and her heart squeezed once more. As Mace walked past her, he reached out, allowing his fingers to trail down her arm, before moving into the den with her son. Standing dumbly in the foyer, her eyes still staring toward the space where the two had disappeared, she finally jerked back to the present. Unable to keep the smile from her face, she moved quickly into the kitchen.

An hour later, the three of them sat at the table,

David and Mace both shoveling lasagna, salad, and garlic bread into their mouths.

"So, when we come in, it sets off the timer to the alarm that would go off just like if a bad guy came in, right?"

Nodding, while chewing, Mace confirmed.

"And we've got thirty seconds to put in the code, so the alarm doesn't go off," David said. His face scrunched for a moment, before he asked, "But, that also means that a bad guy could get into our house and have thirty seconds to do something bad before the alarm goes off, right?"

Her eyes jumped from her son's inquisitive face to Mace, who had just swallowed heavily. She knew David was concerned but had not known how to alleviate all his fears.

Mace brought his napkin to his lips and wiped, thinking furiously of his answer to David's question. Deciding honesty was best, he nodded. "Yes, that's right. But, you have to remember that the security lights will have already gone on when it's dark, and that, right there, will keep most people away. They won't try to enter a house that has that kind of lighting, knowing that there would also be a security system."

David took another bite of lasagna, but Sylvie could see the wheels turning in his head. Her dinner was beginning to sit like a rock in her stomach and she lay her fork down.

Mace, missing nothing, saw her concern. "David," he said, drawing the young boy's attention. "During the day, you're at school, and when you're not, you'll have me, or one of my men, watching you."

David held his gaze, before shifting his eyes to his mother for a second. "But, wouldn't we be safer, if you stayed here at night with us?"

Gasping, Sylvie jerked in her seat. She opened her mouth to refute David's question, but Mace got there before her.

"You're right. And that's why, for the next couple of nights, I'll sit outside and make sure everything is fine."

"David! Mr. Hanover cannot spend the nights in his car! He's given us the security, so we're safe—"

"He can stay in the house with us," David argued. "That way we'll be even safer!"

She opened her mouth to protest, but the look on David's face halted her words. He was trying to be brave, but she saw the fear deep in his eyes.

Mace watched the interaction between mother and son and recognized the emotion in David's eyes as well. "I'll stay." Before he could change his mind, or Sylvie could protest, he added, "I'll stay on the sofa, if the offer still stands."

Sylvie opened and closed her mouth several times, grateful to have Mace's presence nearby and that he cared so much about David's concerns. But, knowing he would be in the house, just one floor below her, would keep her awake all night. Finally, pushing her attraction to him out of her mind, she nodded. "Thank you, for... well," she cleared her throat. "Just...thank you."

He held her gaze for a moment, a slow smile spreading across his face as if he were reading her mind, causing her to blush. With a chin dip and a wink, he went back to eating. David, now smiling widely, began shoveling in his food once more. Swallowing heavily, she picked up her fork and joined them.

That evening, after David had long since been tucked into bed, and she and Mace had spent a few hours watching TV, she rose from her chair, and said, "Let me get a blanket and a pillow."

Mace watched Sylvie turn and walk out of the room. Standing, with his hands on his hips and his head hanging down, he stared at his boots. *What the fuck am I doing?* Before he had a chance to answer his own question, she walked back into the room, a folded blanket and soft pillow in her hands.

He moved toward her, reaching out to take them from her and his hands grazed her fingers. A strange electricity seemed to move between them with their touch and he jerked. She appeared to have felt it also, her eyes jumping to his and her lips parting, ever so slightly.

Dropping the items to the sofa behind him, he stepped forward, placing his hands on either side of her face, his thumbs caressing her cheeks. He saw desire in her eyes, matching his own, and leaned forward, giving her a chance to pull away. Instead, she leaned closer.

Their lips met, his warm and strong, hers cool and trembling. Moving slowly, he angled her head gently while keeping the kiss light.

Sylvie moved her hands to Mace's arms, sliding upward until she clasped his thick shoulders. His kiss reverberated throughout her whole body, warming her, but doing nothing for the trembling, considering she was now shaking with need.

She had no idea how many minutes passed as their arms held each other close and their lips moved over each other's. Want, need, desire—all flew through her. Allowing him to take charge of the kiss, she left no doubt as to how much she wanted this.

Drawing Sylvie closer, Mace felt her curves line up perfectly against the hard planes of his body, but as he felt his erection press into her stomach, he jerked back. Sucking in a ragged breath, he dropped his hands from around her and stepped backward. Her face changed from languid pleasure to confusion as questions formed in her eyes, but he shook his head and moved further away.

"Fucking hell," he mumbled. "I'm sorry...that was so wrong." Hurt slashed across her face and he hated that he had both lost control and kissed her, and that he had stopped the kiss at all.

She lifted her hand to her tender, well-kissed lips. "Wrong? Why?"

For a man who prided himself on knowing the answers, he stumbled trying to explain his conflicting feelings. "You're a client...someone I'm here to protect. You're vulnerable. I shouldn't be...shouldn't have... we shouldn't..."

Suddenly, the look in her eyes changed from hurt and uncertainty, to anger. "That's a lot of *shouldn'ts*, don't you think? After all, I'm not really your client since I'm not paying for any of this. And how dare you say I'm vulnerable. I'm not some helpless, little woman that you have to save. I agree that the situation is unusual and I won't be so stupid as to say I don't need your assistance. But that's not the same as being vulnerable. I'm a full-grown woman who knows her mind and knows what she wants."

Her eyes snapped and color rose over her cheeks, and he couldn't help but think she was more beautiful than ever. "I'm sorry. I didn't mean to imply that you were incapable—"

Huffing, she turned and walked away. Reaching the bottom of the stairs, she halted, her hand on the rail, with her back toward him. Heaving a great sigh, she looked over her shoulder, the light in her eyes pinning him to where he stood. "I'm not the type of woman to throw myself at just any man. In fact, it's been many years since I've felt any desire at all. My life is taking care of David but that doesn't mean that, as a woman, I don't have other feelings. I'm sorry if I made you uncomfortable. I wouldn't want you to do anything that felt *wrong*." Swallowing deeply, she climbed the stairs, tossing out, "Sleep well, Mace."

He stood for a long time in the middle of the room, the blankets and pillow lying untouched on the sofa. Shaking his head, he chastised, *I'm a fucking fool. Not for initiating the kiss... but for stopping it.*

12

Sleep proved elusive, as Mace tossed and turned on the sofa, unable to get comfortable. Knowing Sylvie was upstairs in her bed, he wondered if she were as frustrated as he. Swinging his legs around, he planted his feet on the floor. With his elbows propped on his knees, he rested his head in his hands, digging his palms into his eyes as the morning light began peeking through the blinds on the windows.

He was attracted to her, there was no doubt about that but, the idea that he might be taking advantage of someone in a vulnerable state, ate at him. *No, I did the right thing. I couldn't risk that, no matter how much I want her.* Blowing out his breath, he lifted his head, a grimace on his face, remembering her angry words from the night before.

"I'm not some helpless, little woman, that you have to save... I'm a full-grown woman, who knows her mind and knows what she wants."

The sound of soft footsteps coming down the stairs caught his attention and he looked over just as Sylvie came into sight. Dressed in black yoga pants with a slouchy, pale green T-shirt and her hair pulled up into a sloppy bun, she looked beautiful.

He stood quickly, refusing to give her a chance to avert her eyes. "Sylvie," he called out, watching her nervously glance his way. "How are you?"

She lifted her shoulders in a slight shrug, meeting his eyes. Raising her chin, she replied, "Fine."

"Well, I'm not. I barely slept at all." Her eyes widened and her head tilted slightly to the side.

"I'm sorry," she said, stepping closer, her eyes dropping to the sofa behind him before coming back. "Did you need another blanket? I'm sure a man your size probably wasn't comfortable—"

He shook his head, stalking closer until his bare feet were just in front of hers and her head tilted back to hold his gaze. "I owe you an apology—"

Immediately, her eyes narrowed and she began to turn away. "If you're going to apologize again for that kiss, just stop right now. I—"

He reached out and grabbed her shoulders, gently turning her back to him. Shaking his head, he said, "No. I'm not apologizing for the kiss. I'm apologizing for stopping the kiss."

She held her body perfectly still, his words taking a moment to sink in. Biting her lip, she said, "I'm not sure I understand."

He drew her closer, until their bodies were almost flush once again. "I didn't want to take advantage of you. That was the only reason I stopped the kiss. You need to understand, I wanted to kiss you. I don't see you as a helpless woman. You're a strong woman and a wonderful mother, and I think I've wanted to kiss you since I first laid eyes on you when we ran into each other and you were standing there with my coffee all over your shirt."

Sylvie's mouth fell open, but no words came out. Her heart raced as she watched Mace's face slowly descend toward hers. He stopped, a whisper away from her lips, and she knew he was giving her a chance to back away. Instead, she threw her arms around his neck and pulled him down to her.

Their lips crashed together and, this time, the burn flamed immediately. She rose to her toes and he wrapped his arms around her, lifting her higher. Her legs shot around his waist and he held her easily against his chest.

Tongues tangled, noses bumped, and their lips moved as though they could not get enough of each other. Her breasts swelled and her nipples hardened, almost painfully. She could feel his erection through his jeans, hot against her core. Somewhere in the recesses of her mind, she knew they needed to slow down before David woke up, but she could not bear to break the kiss.

The sound of a car door slamming brought Mace's attention out of the moment and his head jerked away from Sylvie's, eliciting a mewl of discontent from her. "Sorry, sweetheart. Someone's here."

He gently set her back to the floor, his hands on her waist until she was steady on her feet. Stalking to the door, he peered through the peephole, stunned to see her ex-husband on the other side. Whipping his head around, he pierced her with a glare. "You expectin' someone?"

Before Sylvie had a chance to decipher Mace's change in mood, she heard Ed's voice call out as he banged on the door.

"Sylvie!"

Ignoring Mace, she darted around him, opening the door just enough to see through. "What are you doing here? Keep your voice down! I don't want you waking David!"

Ed weaved around slightly, his face hardening. "Come on, Sylvie."

Speaking through the screen door, she said, "You dare to come here when you've been drinking? I told you the last time. No more. You cannot come here and ask for money. I've got nothing left to give you."

Sneering, he said, "Well, then maybe it's time for me to just pay a little visit to David. Let him know how much his father misses him—"

Before she had a chance to respond, the door moved out of her hand as Mace opened it wider. She felt his body right behind her, heat radiating off him as the small space filled with his anger.

Ed's bloodshot eyes widened in shock, for a moment, then narrowed. "Mason? Mason Hanover? What the fuck are you doing in my wife's—"

"Ex-wife," she bit out, before processing that he recognized Mace.

"Doesn't sound like you're welcome here, Ed," Mace growled.

"You always were self-important. Figured you'd be off doing your hot-shit soldier thing." He staggered slightly, clutching the rail to keep from toppling backward. His eyes drifted down to her before moving back up. "You always got everything you wanted. Guess that's why you're here. Can't stand that I had her first."

Mace took a step forward, gently shifting her body to the side, as he ate up all the space. Unlatching the screen door, he walked through, towering over Ed.

Looking less sure, Ed said, "Hey, I'm not looking for any trouble. I just need a little money. Who she's fucking isn't any concern of mine."

Mace's fist darted out, connecting with Ed's jaw, causing him to stumble backward, landing on his ass.

Screaming, she darted out, throwing herself in front of Mace. "Stop! What are you doing? I don't want David to see this!"

Mace's chest heaved, not in exertion, but in frustration.

Sylvie turned and faced Ed as he pulled himself back up, holding his already bruising jaw. "We've been over a long time. For seven years, I've let you take advantage of me because part of me felt sorry for you. But no more. I have full custody and I don't care about your threats anymore. No judge will give you visitation even if you really wanted it. So leave and don't come back."

She turned, shot Mace a withering glare as well and stalked back inside the house, slamming the door behind her.

Anger coursed through Mace, but he forced himself to be calm. Turning Ed toward the road, he escorted him back to the waiting taxi.

"Man, I don't know what the fuck your game is. You had a chance with a wonderful woman and your son. Then you lost that, the first time you took your hand to her."

Falling into the taxi, Ed looked up, his bravado returning. "You always got everything. Anything you wanted, it came your way. Fine," he threw up his hand. "You want her, you've got her. She's not worth the trouble."

As the taxi drove down the street, Mace stood with his hands on his hips, watching it disappear. He turned, looked at the house and, seeing the closed front door, let out a sigh.

Walking back up the porch steps, he tried the doorknob, uncertain if it was locked. Heartened that it turned, he opened it and walked into the house. Hearing noise coming from the kitchen, he moved down the hall.

Sylvie, beating pancake batter into submission, was fuming. Without lifting her eyes, she said, "You know him." It wasn't a question. The truth of the matter was obvious.

"Yes," he replied.

"And you didn't think to tell me."

He retorted, "And you didn't think to tell me that your ex comes by sometimes to hound you for money? To threaten you?"

Her hands stilled and she set the bowl down, turning

to face him. Her blue eyes, now the color of ice, glared. "What? You're angry with me? Are you fucking serious?"

"I'm responsible for your safety. You should have told me. We talked the other night about Ed and his behavior towards you and why you left. That would've been a perfect time for you to let me know that he's still a threat."

Throwing her hands to the side, she faced him fully. "I'm sorry that my mind was occupied with my son being threatened by a possible murderer! I'm afraid that thoughts of my ex-husband rarely come to mind in the face of that." She whirled around, her hair flying about her, and grabbed the bowl of batter.

Neither spoke, for several minutes, as she poured pancakes then stood over them, flipping them more carefully than he expected, given her anger. Finishing, she stacked them on a plate and began frying bacon. It appeared she was preparing to feed an army and he wondered if she was paying attention to what she was doing.

Dropping his chin, he blew out a long breath, pondering what to say. "Sylvie...I'm sorry. Please hear me out."

He waited until she turned around, facing him, but noted her arms were crossed protectively over her middle.

"I knew Ed in boot camp. That's how we met. Didn't care for him when I first met him, but you learn pretty quickly that the Army plans on breaking you down so they can build you back up. They take a group of people, often with little in common, and turn them into a team. Hell, that was just boot camp...nothing like Special Forces training. Ed never tried to conform. He had glorious plans of joining a specialized unit but refused to put in the work necessary to even make it through basic training."

Without saying anything, she turned around and flipped the stove off, putting the cooked bacon onto a paper towel. Facing him again, she leaned her hip against the counter, crossed her arms in front of her, and looked up at him.

"He got through boot camp only because the rest of us hounded his ass. The military believes in group punishment, which meant if he slacked off, we all had to work harder. So, we hauled him along, forcing him to do everything he was supposed to do, so that we could all make it through."

Dragging his hand through his hair, he held her gaze. "I saw you... a couple of times. He used to brag about his gorgeous wife, never saying anything else about you, other than how good you looked on his arm." She winced and he hated that his words caused her pain. Continuing, he said, "He was right, about you being gorgeous. I never got a chance to talk to you, so we never officially met. He seemed possessive and managed to keep you separated, even from the other wives."

"So, when did you realize who I was?"

Closing his eyes, for a few seconds, he knew his next words would probably create a chasm between them, but she deserved honesty.

"Part of what we do, besides being tasked with high-level security, rescues, or investigations, is keep our ear to what we call chatter." Seeing her tilt her head in question, he explained, "We may work internationally a lot, but I'm a firm believer in using our resources locally where we can. So, we listen to what's going on with the local and State Police. I came across the initial report filed after David had been in your office. I was intrigued, but had no real plans of following through, until an update to the report came in. I did a little digging and I recognized you. After a little more digging, I discovered that you were divorced and found myself wanting to help."

She dropped her eyes, turning back to the stove. Within a few minutes she had plated scrambled eggs, bacon, and pancakes loaded with syrup and butter. Pushing the plate toward him, she said, "Here."

He thanked her, feeling guilty that she was not eating, but glad she was not kicking him out of the house. Watching her out of the corner of his eye, she fiddled with the pans in the sink, keeping her eyes averted from him. Expecting David would be getting up soon, he asked, "What about Ed?"

Her delicate shoulders lifted in a slight shrug, and she said, "Everything I told you the other night is true. The only thing I left out was that occasionally he comes by wanting money. I've never given him much, not knowing how it would be spent. I suppose I was always grateful that he gave me the divorce without any hassle. He knew at the time that getting away with no alimony or child support was a huge plus for him. I don't know about his life now and don't care but, I assume that he's hit hard times."

"He threatens you?"

"Not in the way you think. Since that night, he's never threatened me with physical harm. But he has threatened to make life difficult for me by saying he will seek out David. He's even threatened to take me back to court for visitation."

"So, you've given him money over the past seven years."

Nodding, she agreed. "It seemed the path of least resistance." She looked up at him, holding his gaze, and said, "I'm sure, to a man like you, that must be a consideration you've never had to make. But, for me, it was the best thing I could've done at the time."

Just then, they heard the sound of David's feet scuffling upstairs. Looking at each other, no words were spoken, the air crackling between them.

Breathing out, she quickly said, "You may take him to school today, but I won't be going into work. You don't need to come back. I thank you for the security that you put in, but we'll be fine now."

The last bite of food stuck in his throat, but he nodded, her dismissal ringing loud and clear.

13

"See you later," Mace called out as David climbed from his SUV. He watched as the young boy smiled and tossed his hand up in a wave, before jogging toward the school.

He sat for a moment, watching David disappear into the building.

Pulling out onto the crowded street in front of the school, he scrubbed his hand over his face, fatigue settling deep inside. It wasn't the lack of sleep that caused the exhaustion. It was the inner battle he fought over his conflicting feelings about Sylvie.

More determined than ever, he drove out of town and back to the lighthouse. Heading straight to the LSI compound, he nodded at the others already gathered and walked over to Rank.

"Got a favor to ask. Get me everything you can find on Ed Gardner."

"Sylvie Gardner's ex-husband?"

Nodding, he said, "Yeah. He showed up this morning... drunk...and it appears he does that occasionally when he wants money. Threatens to make her life hell with David if he doesn't get it."

"You've gotta be shittin' me," Rank cursed.

"Wish I were. Knew the guy when he was an asshole back in basic and he's worse now. I let him know where he stood this morning but, I've got no illusions that the lesson took hold. I want to know where he is, where he goes, where he lives. He even breathes in their direction, I want to know."

A few of the others, listening to the conversation, nodded in agreement. Babs lifted her eyebrow, and said, "Damn, boss. If I didn't know better, I'd think you've got a real personal stake in this case."

Glaring in her direction, he scowled and she laughed out loud. Turning to the others, he said, "All right, let's get the staff meeting underway."

They gathered around the table, each updating on the cases they had open.

"Nothing new from Ted, our contact at the CIA, on the Honduras situation, but our contact says that the situation there still needs monitoring," Josh reported. "I'm keeping an eye on it, but until we get the official request, there's not much to do."

He nodded, turning toward Tate. "Just finished the identity change for the daughter of the family being threatened by the mob boss. The whole family is moving and we've got the FBI involved with their security as well."

"You get your sister moved?" he asked Walker.

"Yeah, boss. Thanks for the time off. She and her husband appreciate it. I haven't even told you all that I'm gonna become an uncle." The congratulations flowed in and Walker grinned. "I know being pregnant doesn't mean she can't do things, but I couldn't let her lift boxes and move shit."

Mace smiled in return, his heart squeezing at the thought of protecting a sister, but he pushed those thoughts down. Sucking in a deep breath, he turned his attention back to the other reports.

When the meeting came to an end, he settled into a chair next to Rank. Together, they began to look at what they could find on Ed. By lunchtime, they had a full dossier on him and he gave Rank the assignment of keeping track of him.

Grinning, Rank said, "No worries, boss. I'll get to his place and get a tracer on his vehicle this afternoon, as well as keep tabs on his calls for a taxi."

Standing and stretching his arms out to the side, he decided he would have just enough time to work out before going to lunch.

As he moved to walk out of the room, Babs looked up, her eyes wide. "Mace, wait. I've got Detective Martinez on the line."

The group turned and listened as Babs put Roberto on speaker. "Mace? Just wanted to let you know, we found Charles Jefferson's body. Someone tossed it into the city dump. Also, thought you'd want to know…he'd been strangled. And, from the initial report, it looks like it was with a rope…from behind."

Heart dropping, he said, "I need to get to David."

"We can pick he and his mother up—"

"No. They're mine," he rushed, not heeding the double meaning of the words.

"Okay," Roberto agreed. "We're working the murder, but we're trusting our witness' protection to you."

Sylvie spent the morning scrubbing her house from top to bottom. Bathrooms, kitchen, dusting, vacuuming, she even managed to throw in a load of laundry. Frustration coursed through her veins, but the hard, physical labor did little to quell it.

Her thoughts were a tangled web. Her boss was threatening to fire her. Her ex-husband was threatening to take her to court. And out there, somewhere, was an unknown threat because of what her son had witnessed.

And, if all of that was not enough, the infuriating, albeit gorgeous, Mace had taken root in her mind. As angry as she had been that morning, when he put himself between her and Ed, forcing Ed to back down, she also realized she had never had a man do that for her. While it grated on her that he had not mentioned he knew Ed or had seen her before, she had to admit that it did not change what they had now.

Sighing, she took another swipe of the already clean kitchen counter before tossing her rag into the sink in frustration. *How did my life get so out of control?*

The phone rang and she was glad for the distraction. Seeing the school's number on the ID, she hoped David had not gotten sick again. "Hello. This is Ms. Gardner."

Hearing the principal's voice, she startled, her heart pounding.

"Ms. Gardner, this is Mrs. Carnes. I need to let you know that a man just came into the office saying that he was here to speak to David. He claimed it was on official business."

Gasping, she said, "No. No. You didn't let anyone talk to him did you?"

"No. I assure you that David is safe in his classroom."

Wondering if Ed had attempted to see or, God forbid, take David, she asked, "What did he look like? Medium height, light brown hair? I have full custody and his dad is not supposed to—"

"Yes, we know, Ms. Gardner. He did not show us identification, but even if he had, we would not let someone speak to your child without you being present. He was a larger man with dark hair. As soon as we informed him that he would not be able to speak to David, he left hurriedly."

Slumping back against the counter, her heart racing, she said, "Thank you. Thank you. Please keep an eye on David. Do not let him outside, or out of your sight. I'll be there. Give me just a few minutes. I have to get hold of someone, but I'll be there."

"Take your time, Ms. Gardner. David is safe, I assure you."

Disconnecting, her hand shot to her trembling lips as she squeezed her eyes shut, her mind racing. All other thoughts other than David's safety left her mind. Looking down at her phone, held in her shaking hand, she quickly dialed.

The phone rang several times before being answered. Not giving Mace a chance to speak, she plunged ahead. "Someone went to the school, tried to see David. They wouldn't let him and the principal called me. Said the man left. It wasn't Ed. I don't know who it was. Mace, who would try to see him? They didn't show ID—"

"Whoa, Sylvie, slow down. Take a breath and let it out slowly, then tell me what happened." As Mace spoke, he looked up, seeing the others' eyes on him, mirroring his concern.

Sylvie sucked in a gasp, forcing her words to slow as she grabbed her keys and walked toward the door. "I just got a call from David's principal. She said a large man, with dark hair, came in and asked to speak to David. He said it was official, but did not show them any ID. As soon as they told him that a parent would need to be present, he left quickly. They've kept David in his classroom and they're watching him—"

"Where are you now?" Mace asked, heading toward the elevator.

"I'm at home, but I'm getting ready to leave right now. I'm heading to the school."

"No!" he shouted. "That might be exactly what someone's hoping for. They probably knew the school would call you and you may be their target. Stay right there, I'm on my way."

She protested, "I'm not just staying here. My son needs me and no one better get between me and my son! If you want to come, that's fine. I'll meet you at the school." With that she disconnected and grabbed her purse. Stepping out, she set the alarm before shutting the door. Rushing to her car, she made sure to keep her eyes peeled, but saw nothing untoward. Slamming her car door shut, her heart still pounding, she steeled her resolve. *No one threatens my child!*

Arriving at the school ten minutes later, she jumped from her car and raced inside the building. Standing outside the office door, she counted to ten, breathing deeply. Not wanting David to see her upset, she plastered a smile on her face and walked in.

As soon as the principal saw her, she motioned for her to come into her office. Sitting down, she gratefully accepted the water bottle handed to her.

"What on earth is going on?" Mrs. Carnes asked.

Taking a long sip of the cool water, she tried to decide how much information she was allowed to give. Deciding that minimal was best, she replied, "My ex-husband has been a little threatening lately and my fear was that he may have come to the school."

"I assure you, we know that he has no visitation rights and would never let him in to see David. But I don't believe that this man today was your ex-husband."

Fiddling with her purse strap, she said, "Well, I will also say, that we had an incident last week where our house was broken into." She heard Mrs. Carnes gasp, and continued, "I have no idea what anyone would have been looking for, but it still makes me nervous."

"The man said that it was official, so I suppose he could have been from the police," Mrs. Carnes said, but her brow knit and doubt laced her words. "I just don't know why he wouldn't show us his ID."

Shaking her head, she said, "I don't either. But, since this is the last full day of school, would it be all right if I took him with me now? I hate for him to miss the fun of the few half days next week, but I think perhaps I'd like to keep him with me."

Mrs. Carnes nodded in understanding, and said, "I understand. If you would like to go ahead and check him out of school today, that would be fine. I'll let his teacher know and she can simply grade him out for the year." She stood and walked out of her office to the secretary, asking to have David dismissed for the day. Turning as Sylvie came out behind her, she placed her hand on Sylvie's arm, and said, "Please take care of yourself."

She blinked, fighting the tears that threatened to fall, wondering how their lives had become so overwhelming. Swiping her eyes quickly, she smiled as David walked through the door with his backpack. He looked up at her and she recognized confusion mixed with fear.

"Mom? Is everything alright?"

Kneeling in front of him, she wrapped her arms around him, pulling him tightly in for a hug. Forcing lightness into her voice, she replied, "Everything's fine, sweetheart. I was just out this way and thought that I would pick you up from school a little early. Mrs. Carnes said it would be fine for you to come home now."

She listened as he let out a heavy breath. Her heart ached for the fear that he had. Pulling back, she looked at him, his smile now wide.

"Cool! Is Mr. Hanover outside?"

"Uh...no. I just decided to come get you myself." Standing, she took his hand and, with a nod toward Mrs. Carnes, they walked outside. On the way to her car, she heard the squealing of tires and jerked her head around.

Mace's SUV pulled in next to her and she watched as he jumped from the vehicle, slamming his door, before stalking toward them, anger written in the hard set of his jaw. She immediately stepped slightly in front of David, putting her hand on him to gently push him back.

Mace, furious, saw the protective movement and locked down his emotion. Blowing out his breath, he smiled, "Hey, David."

David pushed away from behind his mother and jogged up to him. "Hi Mr. Hanover. Mom picked me up a little early today."

"I see that," he said, placing his large hand affectionately on David's shoulder. Lifting his gaze to Sylvie's, he said, "You ready to go?"

Sylvie's eyes darted to Mace's SUV, where another man was climbing down from the passenger seat. Noting he was handsome, with tattoos showing, a little scruff on his face, and unbelievably fit, she also realized he did not make her pulse race the way Mace did. Curious, she shifted her gaze back to Mace, his hand held out.

"Tate will drive your car back to your house. You and David will ride with me." Seeing her about to protest, he lowered his voice, and said, "Don't fight me on this, Sylvie."

Wanting to rail against his high-handedness, she glanced down at David, peering up at her expectantly. "Sure. That'll be great." After buckling David into the backseat of the SUV, she started to climb in with him when a large hand halted her progress. Twisting her head, she saw Mace close.

"When we get to your house, we need to talk."

As much as she wanted to protest, she knew he was right. Someone had tried to get to David. They were lucky this time and she wanted to keep that luck with her.

14

Sylvie stood inside her living room, staring out the window, her hands clasped tightly in front of her. As soon as they had gotten home, she had sent David off to play, while Mace focused his attention on her. She had assumed he was going to chastise her for leaving the house and going to David's school, but instead he placed his hands gently on her shoulders and held her gaze as he insisted that she and David needed to get away to a safe place.

All of her protestations had faded away as she was reminded of the fear that had gripped her heart when she first got the call from Mrs. Carnes. She had agreed, her head nodding in jerks, but she had no idea where they could go. His mind was working behind his eyes as she stared up into his face, but he remained silent.

With her agreement, he had walked back outside and was now talking to the man introduced as Tate. She watched as he paced, alternating between talking to his co-worker and then talking on the phone.

David came into the room and coming up behind her, said, "Whatcha looking at, Mom?"

She glanced down at him and smiled, ruffling her hand through his hair. "Mr. Hanover would like us to go on a little trip, but I'm not sure where we'll go."

He looked out the window and asked, "Is he going to take us somewhere? Like a vacation?"

She had already explained to him that he would not be going back to school next week for the last three half-days. Knowing he would be missing the end-of-year-party, she had convinced him that they could go somewhere fun.

"I don't know, sweetie." Longing to offer assurances, for once, she had no idea what to tell him. Turning her attention back outside the window, she watched as Mace continued talking to his friend, and wondered if their lives would ever get back to normal.

"Boss, I think you've got the answer staring you right in the face. I just don't know what you're hesitant about." Tate, his hands on his hips, stared at Mace.

He scrubbed his hand over his face before sliding it around to squeeze the tension at the back of his neck. "I need to do this right. I need to keep them safe from whatever threat is out there, but…"

"But, you've got feelings for her."

Surprised, he jerked his eyes up to Tate's.

"Look, Mace. You can fight it all you want, but it's plain to the rest of us that you have feelings for Sylvie. I don't see that there's any conflict of interest here. You've got a place, you've got the room, and they need to get out of here. I think you're making it more difficult than it needs to be."

Blowing out his breath, he planted his hands on his hips. Unable to think of a better plan, he knew he wanted them with him. Nodding, he agreed. "Okay. Let's get them packed up. We'll leave her car here, parked in her garage, and only take our vehicle."

Stepping back inside, he saw Sylvie and David standing in the living room, David looking excited and Sylvie looking as though she might throw up.

"Mom says you're going to take us on a trip!" David piped up, his smile wide.

Grinning in return he said, "Yeah. I've got a great place to take you to, to get away from here for a little while. I just need you two to pack. My friend, Tate, will help."

"Show me to your room, little man," Tate said, as he walked into the house and slid his sunglasses up on his forehead. "We'll make sure to get everything you'll need."

After watching the two of them climb the stairs, Mace swung his gaze back to Sylvie. Walking toward her, he noted her stiff posture. "Look, I know this isn't what you'd like to do, but the danger is getting closer. I can get you to a safe house. I can make sure you and David are out of harm's way."

Saying nothing, she nodded, but began walking past

him toward the stairs. He reached out and grabbed her hand, pulling her gently toward him. Wrapping his arms around her, he rested his chin on her head, feeling her body shiver slightly.

"What about my job?" she whispered. "I've thought about quitting a hundred times, but I don't have that luxury. It pays the bills and—"

"Do you trust me, Sylvie?"

Sylvie leaned her head way back as Mace dropped his chin to peer into her eyes. Allowing his strength to seep into her, warming the places that had grown cold, she nodded. "Yes, I do. In the middle of my world going crazy, I do trust you."

Releasing a breath Mace had not realized he had been holding, he kissed the top of Sylvie's head. "We'll figure this out…together. Go pack your bags, enough for a few weeks, and we'll head out."

Thirty minutes later, with Mace's SUV packed with her and David's suitcases, they pulled out onto the road. Sylvie sat in the back with David and watched the two men in the front. Though they were silent, they appeared to be communicating. She wondered where they were going, but did not ask. She should have realized David would have no such filter.

Bouncing in the back seat, he asked outright, "Where are we going?"

Smiling, as he looked in the rearview mirror, before casting his eyes to the side, toward her, Mace said, "I'm taking you to a place that means a lot to me."

As crazy as it seemed to be driving off toward the unknown, she met his smile. *I've got to treat this like an adventure...at least for David's sake.* Leaning her head back against the headrest, she tried to relax, welcoming the chance to be safe and spending more time with the handsome man at the wheel.

As Mace neared the property, he glanced into the rearview mirror, seeing David's head turned, eagerly looking at the scenery. Glancing over to Sylvie, he observed her eyes were closed, her head gently rocking back and forth against the headrest. *I wonder when was the last time she got a full night's sleep?*

Driving through the forest of Eastern White Pines and Junipers, they finally came out along the coast. He heard David gasp as the view of the ocean could be seen in the distance. He smiled, seeing the enthusiasm on the young boy's face.

Speaking softly, so as not to wake Sylvie, he asked, "Have you spent much time on the water?"

David shook his head, his eyes never leaving the window. "No. We've gone to the beach a couple of times, but that's all."

Driving closer to the coast, his lighthouse could be seen in the distance, but he turned the SUV onto a road just short of it. Driving along a narrow lane, they came to a small cottage, about a hundred feet from the edge of the rocky border of the ocean.

Tate climbed down from the SUV and said, "I'll call someone to come get me while you show them around. We'll help get them settled." With a wink toward David and a two-fingered wave toward him, he moved to the side and pulled out his phone.

Knowing David was itching to get out of the car, he twisted around, reaching between the front seats, placing his hand on Sylvie's thigh and giving a gentle shake. "Hey, we're here."

She blinked her eyes open and looked around, for a moment seeming to forget where she was. Lifting her hand, she pushed her hair back from her face as she looked out the window and spied the small house. White-washed on the outside with a dark brown roof and sporting blue shutters and a blue front door, she exclaimed, "Oh my goodness, is this where we're staying?"

She jerked her head around to him and he smiled and nodded. "It's beautiful, Mace! Absolutely charming!"

"Mom, it looks like something out of a storybook," David exclaimed.

Parking in front, he alighted from the SUV and walked around the front to assist her down, before helping David. "Let's go in and I'll show you around."

Stepping through the front door, that Sylvie noticed Mace had to duck ever so slightly to get through, they moved into an open room, with living room furniture on one side and an open kitchen and dining area on the other. The furniture appeared old, but clean and comfortable. An overstuffed, dark green sofa and two chairs, along with a coffee table and a few lamps, all facing the stone fireplace, filled the living room. Almost as an afterthought was a small, flat screen TV, placed on a wooden table in the corner.

The L-shaped kitchen opened to the space, without a counter to divide it. The table, old, wooden, and scarred, was surrounded by four mismatched chairs.

"Let me show you the rest of the place," Mace invited.

She and David trailed after him, toward the back where there was a large bathroom that included a stackable washer and dryer. A large storage closet was across from that room and she spied the back door leading to the yard toward the cliffs. Opening another door, he showed them a bedroom, furnished with a double bed, dresser, and a small closet. Another door led to the attached full bathroom. Walking to the window, she looked out, seeing a view of the rocky shore and water beyond.

Continuing to follow him, she climbed the stairs, noting again that he had to duck, causing a grin to slip across her face. Once upstairs, she observed two small bedrooms, each containing a twin sized bed and dresser. The ceilings sloped toward the side in each room, but both rooms had a view of the ocean. Another full bathroom stood in between the two bedrooms.

Mace turned toward Sylvie, wondering what she thought of her new accommodations. "It's not much, but it's clean and, most importantly, it's safe—"

She whirled around, placing her hands on his biceps, and said, "It's lovely. Honest, it's perfect."

He smiled, his hands moving naturally to her waist. They stood for a moment, their eyes staring into each other's depths, until a noise behind had them both jumping apart.

"Mom! This is great!"

Sylvie smiled indulgently at David and the three of them moved back downstairs where Tate and another man had unloaded their belongings, placing them in the living room. She thanked them both, after being introduced to Rank. The two men headed out and she turned back toward Mace.

David was busy unpacking his iPad, and Mace moved her to the side so they could speak privately.

"This place is safe, off the grid. I'm close by and can be here in a moment's notice." He handed her a phone, and said, "This is what's known as a burner phone. You'll use it for now and then we'll get rid of it. But, unless you're calling for me, I don't want you to use it. I've got to head out...I've got my men looking into who came to the school today."

At that reminder, the smile dropped from her face, the reality rushing back at her that this was no vacation, but a hideaway. Nodding silently, she waited for more instruction.

"I'll stop by this evening, to make sure you've got everything you need."

"We're good, Mace. I want to thank you for everything you're doing for us—"

He stepped closer, lifting his hand to cup her face. "No thanks are needed. I want you safe...I want David safe. Don't worry, we're going to get these guys and you can have your life back."

Filled with peace since stepping into the house, she

was struck with the idea that she might not want her old life, with her old job, and with threats from Ed, to come back. *But if I don't have my old life, what will I have?*

Interrupting those thoughts, Mace bent and kissed her lips gently before walking out of the room, leaving her staring in his wake.

15

Stepping out of the elevator and into the main room of the compound, Mace stalked straight to Josh. "What have you got?"

"Looking at the traffic cams, it's taking a bit of time. It's been a long time since I've been around an elementary school, but the number of cars coming and going to the school is incredible. Not knowing if the man parked and went there directly, or had been sitting there for a while, I'm combing through the ones since that morning."

"Anything show up?"

Nodding, he replied, "Finally, got a lock on a car registered to Thomas Perdue. With a little bit of searching, I determined that he has no children and would have no reason to be at that school. With a bit more digging, I see that he, at one time, worked for the Crossover Building Company."

"Good work," he said, starting to walk away.

"There's more," Clay added, gaining his attention. "Searching into the background of Thomas Perdue, we've also seen his name as an employee of the National Supreme Endeavor Group."

"Finally!" he exuded. "A connection between the two. Good work. Get it to Martinez."

The group moved to the table in the middle of the room and began comparing notes.

Cobb began, "I talked to Detective Martinez this morning and he said that he interviewed Doug Smiteson, the owner of the Crossover Building Company. This is the company that's constructing the high-rise where the assault took place."

"Anything from him?"

Cobb shook his head, "No. The man appeared shocked and distressed that something had happened in the building. When he was shown a picture of the man in the construction vest and hardhat from Ms. Gardner's phone, he claimed that was not one of his construction workers."

He thought for a second, before looking up, "How large is his building company?"

With a few strokes on the keyboard, Cobb said, "It has building projects all over the state. Permanent employees are listed at a little over three hundred. Then contract employees make up almost another thousand."

"How the hell could the owner claim to know what all those people look like?" Josh asked. "No way would he know all those people, especially not at first glance at a picture. Sounds like he was just going to deny whatever he saw."

"How are we with the list of registered members of the NSEG?" he asked.

"Frustrating as hell," Bray breathed out. "We can get our hands on the list of donors easily, but because they don't charge a membership fee, per se, we can't find a list of who might belong."

Walker added, "And they don't have formal meetings anywhere either. What I'm starting to work on is their email list."

Mace glanced sharply his way, and asked, "Wouldn't an email list be easy to dig into?"

Nodding, Walker agreed. "Yeah, but this is no fly-by-night group. Looking into their history, they've been around for a long time. And they've got money. Serious money. Don't worry, boss, we'll hack into their list, but I've got to tell you that they've spent a small fortune in covering up who their members are."

"Probably protecting some wealthy and politically connected members," Drew surmised.

"Hmph," Tate groused. "Supremists know it's not politically correct to be associated with a group, but don't have any trouble feeding their money into the organization."

Bringing them back to the task, he ordered, "Once you get in there, see if you can dig up any recent ties between Thomas Perdue and Doug Smiteson, and anything at all between the Crossover Building Company and the NSEG."

From across the cavernous room, Babs yelled, "Detective Martinez wants to know if you'd like to accompany him when he goes to talk to Richard

Atkins?" Seeing his head tilt, she explained, "He's the head of the NSEG."

"Tell him abso-fucking-lutely," he replied. "It'll give me a chance to eyeball the inside of their building." Grinning, he added, "Who knows, gentlemen? We might just need to make a little nighttime visit."

"Hello?"

Sylvie looked up at a knock on the front door before it was unlocked and opened, an older woman sticking her head in. Eyes wide, she stared, unsure if anyone was supposed to drop by, even if they did have a key. The woman had thick, grey hair, cut in a short bob and blue eyes that immediately fastened onto her.

"Um…hello?"

David came careening into the room, but halted as she threw her arm out to stop him. Stepping partially in front of him, she maintained her protective stance.

The older woman's gaze dropped to David before lifting back to her, a smile curving her lips. "Well, hello there. Sorry if I frightened you. I'm a friend of Mace's. My name is Marge. Marge Tiddle."

A grey-haired man with bushy eyebrows stepped in behind Marge and she introduced him as well. "This is my husband, Horace. We help run the lighthouse up the coast."

"I saw it!" David announced, excitement in his voice.

"Shh," she hushed, looking back at the two strangers. Just then her phone rang and she looked down at the screen, seeing Mace's number. Still staring at the two interlopers, she brought the phone to her ear. "Hello?"

"Hey," Mace replied. "I wanted to let you know that my…uh…associates, Marge and Horace Tiddle, are coming by to meet you and David."

Her breath left her body in a whoosh and her heartbeat steadied. "They're here."

Hearing her nervousness, he said, "Oh, Sylvie, I'm sorry I didn't call you earlier. I'm on my way out of town, but I'm glad they're there. You can trust them to take care of you."

"Thank you. You've done so much…but…thank you."

"I'll talk to you later. I'll come by and see you when I can."

She disconnected, then turned a tremulous smile toward the couple still standing in the doorway. Before she had a chance to speak, Marge stepped forward, her hand out in greeting.

Marge grinned and said, "I take it that's Mace? Just like him to wait too late to let you know we're coming. Horace and I wanted to come by and check on you and David, make sure you felt welcome, and to see what you might need."

The older woman's handshake was firm, yet warm. Smiling back at her, she said, "Thank you. That's nice of you to check on us."

David peeked out from behind her hips, smiling up at the two visitors. "Hi! I'm David."

"Well, how do you do, young man?" Horace asked, wiggling his eyebrows.

Marge laughed, and said, "Now that you know it's okay for us to be here, we can get to know each other."

Still in certain of what to say, she simply nodded. Looking around, she waved her hand toward the living room, and said, "Would you like to sit?"

"I'll go get the food," Horace said, turning toward the doorway again. Looking over his shoulder at David, he said, "Would you like to help me, son?"

David turned his face up toward her and she gave a quick nod. Ruffling his hair, she watched as he darted after Horace and the two walked outside. Unable to help herself, she followed to the doorway, watching as they moved to an old truck. Horace was lifting some grocery bags from the back, handing them to David, who was chatting the whole time.

Marge moved silently next to her, placing her hand on her shoulder. "They'll be fine," she assured. "Horace is good with kids, and he knows what David has been through."

At that pronouncement, she jerked her head to the side and stared at Marge. "You know?"

"We don't just take care of the lighthouse. We take care of Mace and the ones who work for him."

Sucking in a deep breath before letting it out slowly, she said, "This is all so much for me to take in. I feel as though my life has turned completely upside down in the last week."

"I brought some muffins. Let me put the kettle on and we can have a nice cup of tea." Marge walked into the kitchen and, looking over her shoulder, said, "I always think everything's better with a nice cup of tea.

Of course, a little whiskey in the tea never hurt, either." Almost as an afterthought, she threw out, "And, if I lack tea, then a straight shot of whiskey always does the trick."

A chuckle slipped from Sylvie's lips and she moved into the kitchen with Marge. Soon the three adults had cups of tea and David had a glass of fresh milk that the Tiddles had brought. She was amazed at how much food they had provided. The refrigerator, freezer, and pantry were now well-stocked.

It made her wonder how long Mace expected her and David to stay in the safe house, but she did not want to ask in front of David.

After finishing his tea and seeing that David had finished his milk, Horace asked, "How would you like to step outside with me, David? We can take a look at the water, the rocks, and I can make sure you know where it's safe to play and where it's not."

Once more, David looked at her and she smiled and nodded. "Thank you, Mr. Tiddle. I would appreciate it if you can make sure he's safe."

With a wink, Horace stood, and said, "That's what we're here for, Ms. Gardner."

Watching as Marge bustled about the kitchen, she said, "I can't thank you enough for what you and your husband have done. When Mace hurried us out of my house, I didn't even think about where we were going or what I might need to bring. I certainly never thought about food."

Marge walked over and patted her hand, saying, "Don't worry about a thing. We'll make sure you have what you need. And, if you think of anything else, just let us know. The closest town is not too far and we run in for supplies all the time."

She and Marge settled in the living room with a second cup of tea and, for the first time in days, she felt herself relax.

"Do you know Mace well?" she asked, dropping her eyes to her tea, hoping her question sounded casual and did not reveal the pounding of her heart.

"I've known Mace for years," Marge admitted. Smiling, she said, "I used to work for a government agency and met him when he was still with the Special Forces. We developed a bond…he was the son I never had and I was the mother he lost. Horace was in the Navy and we both retired from our positions, but found civilian life to be rather mundane."

Marge's smile widened, memories moving across her face. Leaning forward, Sylvie found herself wanting to glean every bit of information about Mace as she could gather. "So, when did you start working for him?"

"I'll let him fill you in on his business as he sees fit, but let's just say that as soon as we found out he was developing his own security company, Horace and I wanted to be nearby. Not that we do any of the security, but just to assist any way we can. Horace helps take care of the physical location and I think of myself as the honorary mom to the employees."

She cocked her head to the side, wondering about the strange career change, blushing as it appeared Marge had noticed her surprise.

Chuckling, Marge said, "You're curious about my

post-retirement career...I suppose it does seem extreme. I had my time being in the thick of things in the field. Now? I prefer to take care of the younger ones who are at the stage in their careers where the action can take precedence over everything else."

"Wow," she breathed, her heart warmed to the giving woman next to her. Before she had a chance to ask more, there was a knock at the door and, just as with Marge and Horace, it was opened before she could reach it. Jumping up, she stared at the beautiful woman walking in. With her athletic build and short, pixie hair, she was striking.

"Hey, I'm Babs. You must be Sylvie."

"Hi," she greeted, unsure about the newest visitor, who smiled as she moved past her and walked into the living room.

"Hey, Marge. I heard you and Horace were over here so I wanted to come meet Sylvie as well." Turning toward her, Babs said, "I'm the administrative manager for Mace's business." Leaning forward, she whispered loudly, "Quite frankly, sometimes there's too much testosterone for any sane female to take. When that happens, I go find Marge to get my estrogen level back on course!"

A giggle slipped from her lips at Bab's description and she immediately determined that she wanted to get to know the irrepressible woman.

"We were just having some tea...will you join us?"

Babs plopped down in one of the chairs and said, "Don't mind if I do."

Marge, peering at Babs, grinned. "Are you sure you

didn't just come to check out the woman that has Mace tied up in knots?"

Her eyes widened at Marge's question, then popped even wider at Bab's response.

"Hell, yeah. I've been waiting for a couple of years for the big man to finally fall for someone."

"Oh, I'm sure you're mistaken," she objected. "He's just being nice, that's all."

Babs and Marge smiled, their faces showing indulgence.

"Well, that would be disappointing," Babs quipped. Softening her voice, she explained, "Mace is a true rescuer...I think it's in his DNA. But, if ever a man needed to have someone special to share his life with...it's him."

"Oh," she breathed, unable to think of anything else to say. "I don't know...well, I'm not sure that we're...I guess..."

Marge leaned forward, patting her arm, saving her from trying to form a response. "Right now, you focus on letting Mace do his job and keep you and David safe. You can figure out what the two of you are later."

Grateful for the understanding, she nodded, sipping her tea as Babs and Marge entertained her with tales of working in their *field of testosterone*.

As the afternoon wore on, she realized it had been a long time since she had felt so relaxed and had laughed so much.

16

Mace looked at the man in the driver's seat as they pulled up outside the brick and glass modern building of the NSEG. Roberto had worked with him and LSI before. Short, stocky, with dark hair cut in a military hairstyle, he exuded quiet control, but was a force to be reckoned with.

Roberto glanced out the window and said, "Not too shabby a place for their non-profit."

His eyes followed Roberto's line of sight and he nodded. "You got that right. And in there, you're in charge, I'm just along for the ride."

Roberto jerked his head to the side, pinning him with his stare. "You think I'm buying that? Don't think I don't know you're scoping out this place." Then, as an afterthought, he jerked his hand up, and said, "But don't tell me what the fuck you're planning. Everything I get, I get through channels that'll hold up in court."

"You know I won't fuck that up. What I find, I'll get

to you, then you can do with it what you need. Your job is to find Charles' killer. My job is to keep Sylvie and David safe. We both know those two things are tied together, but I'll stay out of your way as long as I can keep them from harm."

Roberto nodded before climbing out of his official SUV. Together, they walked through the tall, glass, front doors and into a large lobby. The white tile floors gleamed and the modern, chrome and leather furniture gave off a cold impression to him. A counter was in front of them, with an attractive, well-dressed, young woman sitting behind it. Directly behind her, standing, was a burly security guard.

"Good morning," the perky woman chirped, her smile wide. "How may I help you?"

Roberto pulled out his badge, making sure the security guard saw it as well, and stated, "I'm here to speak to Richard Atkins."

She blinked, her smile never leaving her face, and said, "I'll check to see if he's available—"

"He'll be available. This is an official inquiry."

The young woman remained seated as the security guard said, "Follow me." He moved swiftly toward the elevator, not looking behind to see if they were with him. Entering through the open doors, the guard turned around and he and Roberto stepped in.

Mace adopted a bland expression on his face, but his eyes were already categorizing everything he saw. There were two security cameras in the lobby and the door had basic security alarms. There was no code needed to enter the elevator and the guard had simply pressed for the fourth floor, the top floor of the building. Stepping out of the elevator, they followed the guard to the left and he noted several offices on either side of the hall. Again, no obvious security measures on this floor either.

Stopping at the door on the end, the guard grunted, "Wait here," then, stepped inside the room, closing the door behind him.

Roberto looked up at him but neither one of them said anything, their gazes speaking volumes between them. The guard opened the door and grunted, "Come in."

Walking inside, Mace noted a large, expansive office, with the same modern feel as the lobby. The man sitting behind the desk stood with a smile spread across his face. His salt and pepper hair was slicked back, trimmed neatly. He recognized the expense of the man's suit and at a swift glance noted impeccable grooming as well, from his shave, to buffed nails, to polished shoes.

"Detectives, what a surprise. I'm Richard Atkins. Welcome to the National Supreme Endeavor Group. Please, please, have a seat."

He and Roberto sat in the two chairs facing the desk and he noted the security guard had once more shut the door, now standing on the inside. Roberto introduced the two of them and immediately began.

"I'm sure you've heard of the murder of State Attorney Charles Jefferson. We're investigating and, at this time, are looking for any information that we can gather."

"I understand," Richard said, his voice smooth. "I'm not sure how I can help, though."

"One of the things Mr. Jefferson was working on was looking into your organization."

Unflappable, Richard said, "I can't imagine why he was looking into us, although any group that attempts to limit governmental control is often feared by some and championed by others. I'm sure you must have many organizations you are looking at."

Nodding, Roberto said, "Our investigation is comprehensive, I assure you. I'd like to know who in your organization knew that the State Attorney had an open case on the NSEG?"

"I wouldn't have any records on that. I, myself, have had a conversation with Mr. Jefferson. I'm fairly certain at least one of our board members has also. But it is not something that would be common knowledge here at our group."

"When Mr. Jefferson and you had your conversation, did he inform you of the depth of his investigation?"

Mace watched as Richard, seeming cool and collected, continued to answer Roberto's questions, deftly deflecting each one. Discretely scanning the room while he listened, he noted a security camera in the corner and that the windows were covered in a reflective film, keeping out prying eyes. A bookcase lined the wall to the left and, analyzing the dimensions of the room, he realized it was narrower than the building. Curious, he wanted to know what was behind the wall.

Bringing his attention back to Richard, he listened as the man gave a well-practiced speech.

"I certainly understand that when any non-profit ventures into the political foray, it can make some nervous. But, I assure you, our political views and stance are well documented. We are also largely supported by many Americans who feel the same way we do. Our records are impeccable and were certainly shared with Mr. Jefferson. I had not heard any more from his office and assumed that we were no longer under investigation."

"Had you heard of his disappearance?"

Shaking his head, a concerned expression etched onto his face, Richard said, "No, I had not. It was not until yesterday that I was made aware of the news of his death. I cannot imagine that his demise had anything to do with us."

Several minutes later, he and Roberto walked out of the building and into the sunshine. Sliding his sunglasses on his face, he turned back to stare at the building. Saying nothing, he climbed into Roberto's SUV, then requested, "Need you to circle the building."

Roberto simply nodded, not questioning his reasons. Driving around the block, he confirmed what he already knew. Something was behind the bookcase wall in Richard's office.

Driving away, Roberto slid his eyes toward him, and asked, "Do I even want to know what you're planning?"

Grinning, he just shook his head. "Best, right now, if you just stick to your investigation and let me handle the dirty work."

Sighing heavily, Roberto nodded. "Don't keep me in the dark whenever you find what you suspect."

"You know I won't."

As they continued down the road, he found his mind not only on the upcoming nocturnal visit to the NSEG, but drifting more and more to the beautiful woman that was back at the house.

Ever since Babs, Marge and Horace left, David incessantly talked about the history of the house, the nearby lighthouse, lighthouse keepers, and the rocks leading to the ocean. "Did you know there used to be pirates here, Mom?"

Sylvie, torn between feeling happy that David had something to focus on besides the events of the last week and anxiously glancing out the window wondering if Mace was going to come by, tried to pay attention to what he was saying. "Is that right?" she replied.

Tearing her eyes away from the window, she moved into the kitchen and opened the refrigerator. Marge had certainly done an exceptional job of supplying food. Not only had she filled the refrigerator with groceries, but she had several premade meals ready.

Pulling out a macaroni and cheese casserole that she felt certain David would eat, she placed it in the microwave. Just as she was about to interrupt his constant monologue to tell him to wash up, she heard a vehicle on the gravel out front.

David jumped up, racing to the door, but she halted him with a sharp order. "David! Do not open that door until I have a chance to see who's there!"

She peeped through the hole, her breath catching in her throat as she spied Mace standing just outside. Her heartbeat sped up and she threw open the door. Feeling foolish at her youthful excitement, she said, "I'm glad to see you. Come on in."

"Mom's heating up some of Mrs. Tiddle's macaroni and cheese," David said excitedly. "You're just in time!"

Mace's gaze dropped from Sylvie's face down to David's excited one, and he grinned. "Sounds good." He lifted his gaze back up to Sylvie's, and added, "If that's a real invitation."

She met his smile, and replied, "Absolutely. We'd love to have you." Looking down at David, she shooed him out of the room to wash up. As soon as he was gone, she turned back to him, and said, "This is truly a lovely place for us to stay and I don't want you to think I'm ungrateful." Seeing his brows lower in question, she hurried to continue, "It's just that I wondered how long we might have to stay."

He walked over and gently placed his large hands on her shoulders, feeling tension underneath his fingers. Massaging them, he said, "I know this has all been such a mess for you, but I promise I'm working as hard as I can to neutralize the threat against David."

"I know and I'm so grateful. I know you have men working on this, and Marge and Horace came by today bringing so much food. There's just no way I can pay everyone back—"

He lifted her chin with his knuckle, staring deeply into her eyes. "I can't explain what makes you and David different from other cases that we've had," he admitted honestly. "But I can't stand the thought of you not being here, close by, where I know you're safe."

The ding of the microwave was met with David running back into the room, his clean hands held up for Sylvie to see. Laughing, she stepped back away from him and served up the casserole.

The meal was short in duration but Sylvie felt the nervous tension that had filled her being for a week finally ebbing. David regaled Mace with all of the stories Horace had told him, even though she felt sure Mace knew them by heart. Stories of pirates, lighthouse keepers, and rescuers. She watched David soak up the male attention and prayed it was not something he would get used to and be devastated when it was gone.

Mace cleaned his plate and leaned back in satisfaction. He looked over at Sylvie and David, recognizing how much he enjoyed the time with them. Knowing he needed to head back to LSI for their nighttime reconnaissance, he pushed his chair back and picked up his plate.

David jumped up, saying, "No, let me."

Thanking him, he said, "I've got to go, now, but I'll be back tomorrow. If there's anything you need, you've got Marge and Horace's numbers. Don't be afraid to use them."

Sylvie walked Mace to the door, but he linked fingers with her and pulled her gently onto the porch.

She lifted her face, staring at his square jaw with the dark stubble giving him a dangerous air.

"My men and I have somewhere to be tonight," he said, "but I'll be back tomorrow. Stay here. Stay safe."

She nodded, concerns and questions swirling about her. Mace leaned down, his kiss light at first. She moaned softly into his mouth and he pulled her body flush against his, taking the kiss deeper. Electricity crackled between them as their tongues met and vied for dominance. He plundered her mouth, memorizing the taste and essence of her.

With no space between their bodies, Sylvie pressed tighter, flattening her breasts against his hard chest. Her hands clutched his shoulders as her knees threatened to give out. Just as she was ready to beg him to take her to bed, she felt a rush of cold air between them.

Pulling away from her, Mace regretted the loss of her lips on his. *Damn, what is this woman doing to me?* With his hands cupping her face, he kissed her lightly one more time before heaving a great sigh. "You make leaving so hard to do."

"And you make watching you go, just as hard," she said, her hands still clinging. Swallowing deeply, she forced her fingers to relax, dropping them to his waist with a sigh.

Tilting her head, he kissed her forehead before turning and jogging to his SUV, calling out, "Stay in and stay safe. I'll see you tomorrow."

Driving the half-mile back to the lighthouse, he found it hard to think about the upcoming mission. *Can*

I afford this kind of distraction? Is a relationship ever going to work with the job I have?

No answers to those questions came to him as the sun finally sank into the horizon and night descended. Stalking into the lighthouse, he headed down to the compound, forcing thoughts of Sylvie to the recesses of his mind.

"Bingo."

Mace, sitting in the van with Josh, grinned. Listening to Rank, he knew they had found something. When he had gotten back to the compound, he discovered that Rank had already pulled up the schematics for the building, both what was on file in City Hall and what Mace had called in. The two did not match, so they knew something interesting must lay behind the bookshelf in Richard's office.

Josh had been busy deciphering the NSEG's computers and databases, while Drew looked into their security. Discovering they had more security than what it appeared, Drew grinned at him, saying, "Ain't nothin' we can't bypass undetected."

Now, he and Josh were manning the equipment in the van, both security and computers, as Rank, Tate, and Walker moved into the building.

"What have you got?"

"The room back here is filled to the brim with computers and records. Looks like there are lists of donors and contacts. What's fucking nuts, is that a lot of it's in paper form, not electronic database."

"Easy to shred…not as easy to trace, as long as they keep it under wraps."

"And easier to use as blackmail, if needed, with their wet signatures on the papers."

Josh looked over, and said, "I'll bet they've got the data stored in a server somewhere, just not here, connected to their organization. I'll do more searching when we get back."

"While Walker and I search here, Tate's in Richard's office, looking around."

Clay, back at the compound, came across the radio. "No worries, the security is bypassed."

Another hour passed before the three slipped out as unnoticed as they went in. Once inside the van, they headed back to the lighthouse.

Rank said, "I used the high-speed, digital scanner that Josh rigged and managed to copy what looked the most important."

From the driver's seat, Josh replied, "Good. I'll start work on their hidden server when we get back."

Mace looked at Tate, and asked, "Anything in his office?"

"Fucker's office is so clean it could be a surgical room in a hospital. Even his appointment book was boring as hell." Chuckling, he added, "But, using an old-fashioned, completely non-technical method, I managed to grab a few notes that he had taken."

Walker barked out a laugh and shook his head. "No

fucking way you used a pencil rubbing on a pad of paper."

Tate continued to grin as he looked down at the paper in his hand. "Josh may have all the fancy tricks but I learned a few things from my grandpa."

He took the paper and looked down at it, seeing a name scribbled near the top. "Jonathan Adams. 9 a.m. That's not a name I recognize."

"As soon as we get back," Josh said, "I'll start running some of this through."

He nodded, knowing his men would easily work through the night. Shaking his head, he said, "Only do tonight what has to be done, then get home. Rest and come back, first thing in the morning, ready to tackle this."

His men nodded and he leaned back in his seat, allowing his mind to settle back on Sylvie. *It's their first night in the house. Maybe I should go by and just make sure everything's okay.* Even as the thought crossed his mind, he knew that it was just an excuse. What he really wanted to do, was see her again.

17

"Is he asleep?"

Sylvie nodded, stepping back to allow Mace to enter. Closing the door behind him, she flipped the lock, then looked up at him and blushed. "I suppose I don't need to be so cautious when you're here with us…it's just habit."

Mace looked at Sylvie, all soft and feminine in her robe, belted at her waist, with slippers on her feet. Her hair was down, waving about her shoulders, and the worry lines that had been evident on her face ever since he first saw her, appeared to have eased.

He reached his hand up, tucking a lock of hair behind her ears, and said, "It's a good habit to have."

As she led him into the living room, she said, "In answer to your question, yes. David actually went to sleep fairly easily. I was worried about him being in a new bed, in a new house, with everything going on." Lifting her shoulders in a slight shrug, she smiled. "But, it seems this place agrees with him. Or, maybe it's because Horace came back over and they played in the yard."

Settling on the couch, as close as he could with his body angled so that it was facing her, he nodded. "Horace is a good man."

"He said that he wanted to take David out in a boat." Her eyes were wide as she looked at him for assurance that this was a good plan.

Chuckling, he said, "He'll be in good hands with Horace. He won't let anything hurt David. When I was a child, my grandfather took me out in the boats, told me stories of pirates, lighthouse keepers and rescuers, and showed me the caves around here. Those are some of my best memories."

Sylvie leaned back into the cushions, observing the smile on Mace's face. "That sounds lovely. I suppose you've already guessed that David is desperate for male attention. I've been both mom and dad for so long, that sometimes I forget how much he needs another male. I hope that Horace doesn't get overused." She also hoped that Mace did not feel overused either, but hated to mention it, in case he felt obligated.

He placed his large hand on her leg, his thumb gently rubbing. "Sylvie, any man should feel honored to be around David." She scoffed and he added, "His father's an asshole and he's the one who's missing out."

She snorted softly and said, "I know. I happen to think you're right. It's Ed's loss that he's not in David's life, but it was the best thing for me to have left him. In my opinion, no father is better than an abusive one."

Shifting forward Mace moved closer, smiling as

Sylvie leaned toward him as well. Her face, only a few inches from his, filled his view.

Her large, blue eyes held his, and she asked, "Mace? What are we doing?"

"You were right," he said. "I tried to fight the attraction, feeling as though I was pushing you at a time when you were vulnerable. But, I know what I want and as long as you want the same thing, then I'm ready to take this further. I want to see where we can go."

She closed the slight space between them, her lips meeting his, and she wrapped her arms around his neck. Angling his mouth, his arms around her waist, he pulled her body over onto his lap.

Tonight, Sylvie wanted more, demanded more. Her fingers dug into Mace's shoulders, the thick muscles taut underneath her hands. It had been a long time since she had given in to a sexual urge and the tinder quickly caught fire.

Mace thrust his tongue into Sylvie's warm, silky mouth, exploring every texture and taste, a shock of lust spearing straight through him. He was torn between wanting the kiss to last for hours and wanting to get her naked and under him as quickly as possible.

His hand slid to the front of her robe, parting the lapels and slipping inside, cupping her full breast. His thumb scraped over her nipple, already peaked. She moaned and the sound nearly undid him as he continued to work his tongue and fingers at the same time.

Sylvie arched her back, pressing her breast into Mace's palm further. Her nipples ached with want as she slid her hands forward, cupping his square jaw. "Bed," she mumbled, her lips never leaving his.

He lifted his head to peer into her eyes and asked, "David?"

She inhaled, her breath shuddering in her chest, as she held him tightly. "He's upstairs…asleep." She watched as uncertainty moved across his eyes and she squeezed his face, bringing it inches from hers. "I want this. I want you. Please…don't make me beg, although I will if that makes a difference." She watched in fascination as his hard face melted into a smile.

"Oh, babe, I want this…and you." He stood, effortlessly lifting her into his arms, stalking down the hall to the bedroom.

Lowering her feet to the floor, he gently shut the door, pushing in the doorknob lock, just in case David awoke. Turning back, he watched as she unbelted her robe and allowed it to slip from her shoulders.

Her nightgown was simple…a light pink, sleeveless cotton gown with lace around the bodice. She swallowed hard, realizing that her thirty-year-old, mom's body was not nearly as tight as when she was younger and the male specimen in front of her was at his physical prime.

Refusing to give in to self-doubt, she slipped the gown over her head and dropped it to the floor. Now, clad in only her white, lacy panties, she faced him.

Mace stared at the woman in front of him, her curves enticing, her skin glowing, her hair flowing about her shoulders, and her eyes shining up at him.

Unable to believe this amazing woman was offering herself to him, he was humbled.

Closing the distance between them, he wrapped his arms around her again, pulled her close and dropped his head to kiss her. No longer hesitant, he plundered her mouth, licking, nipping, sucking, thrusting. She clung to his arms as though, without that anchor, her legs would give out.

He moved forward, backing her until she was at the bed and with a gentle push she lay, spread out like a feast to be savored. He bent to take off his boots, then grabbed the back of his shirt, jerking it over his head, before shucking off his pants and boxers.

Sylvie leaned up on her elbows, staring at the male perfection in front of her. Huge, thick muscles covered his chest, arms, torso, thighs. His skin was tanned and, with his dark, black hair and thick scruff, she felt power exuding from his body. He had thick hair on his chest and it tapered to his groin, where his cock jutted out, firm and eager. No artifice…just pure, raw masculinity.

He leaned forward and snagged her panties, dragging them down her legs. Kneeling, he spread her thighs with his shoulders and before she could breathe, he latched onto her clit with his mouth. Throwing her head back in shock, she writhed as he worked magic with his tongue and teeth.

"Oh, my God," she moaned, her fingers moving through his hair. The soft, thick hair against her fingers was in stark contrast to the abrasion of his beard against her inner thighs, but she was unable to decide which felt better. Her body wound tighter as he licked her folds, nibbling on her clit once again.

Mace loved the taste of her, the feel of her. He loved watching how her body opened for him, yielding to his ministrations. Reaching up, he tweaked her taut nipple, rolling the bud between his fingers. Her back arched and she pressed her hot core against his face. Blowing his breath over her sex, he felt her clench against his tongue.

Sylvie clapped one hand over her mouth to stifle her groan, just as her orgasm sent shock waves throughout her body. Sparks lit behind her closed eyelids and as she slowly returned to earth, she was barely aware of him crawling up her body, planting kisses along her skin as he moved from her legs, to her belly, to her breasts.

Latching onto a nipple, Mace sucked the hard peak deeply, grunting with pleasure as she writhed again underneath him. Aware of his heavy body, he settled his weight on his forearms, planted on either side of her. Lavishing attention on each breast, he sucked and nipped, until her fingers dug into his scalp and she moaned her demands. Moving higher, he kissed her again, silencing her, determined to take his time.

"Please, Mace, I need you now."

He lifted his head and stared at the beauty beneath him. Grinning, he said, "Tell me exactly what you want." He watched the adorable blush move from her chest to her cheeks. Nuzzling her nose, he said, "Tell me."

Embarrassed, Sylvie hated that it had been so long that she was desperate, and that she lacked the light sex-talk he was probably used to with his partners. She dropped her eyes, staring at his chin.

He sensed the change in her and shifted down to capture her eyes with his. "Hey…what happened? If you don't want this, we'll stop—"

"No," she rushed, her gaze imploring. "I don't want us to stop…it's just…um…it's been awhile…you need to know that I haven't been with a man since I left Ed—"

"Shh," he hushed softly, not wanting her ex-husband's name or memory encroaching on her thoughts. He cupped her face, his thumbs caressing her cheeks. "I only want to do what you're comfortable with. There's no one else in this bed but you and me. I want this…I want you. And, please babe, understand… this is no fuck. This is the start of you and me…if you'll have me."

The weight on Sylvie's heart lifted as she dragged air into her lungs, letting it out slowly. A smile curved her lips and she nodded. "Yes…I want us."

He kissed her gently, teasing her lips open before plunging his tongue inside once more. Lost in the swirls of emotion, she barely noticed as he rolled to the side to grab the condom he had taken from his pants and tossed to the bed. Before she knew it, he was back on top, his hips settled between her thighs and his thick cock nudging her sex.

"Yes," she breathed, her voice barely recognizable to her ears.

With a swift plunge, Mace seated himself fully in her warm, tight channel, the sensation rocking him to his core. Though he rarely trolled for one-night stands, sex had always been casual to him, having never found anyone he wanted to spend time with. This…now…he could not remember ever feeling the sense of completeness he felt now at their joining.

Wanting her comfortable, he searched her face to assure himself that she was ready. The smile on her lips nearly undid him.

Her eyes, pinned on him, shined as she nodded. More than willing to accommodate, he began to move, slowly at first and then with more vigor. The friction built and he wondered if he would be able to last long enough to bring her to orgasm again.

Sylvie clutched Mace's shoulders before gliding her hands up and down his back. The play of muscles, bunching and cording underneath her fingertips, gave proof to the power in his body. And yet, he moved in her so gently, as though handling delicate china. As his body rocked into hers, she gave herself completely to him.

He felt the second she yielded and knew that the strong woman in his arms was giving all she had to him. Not just her body, but her trust. Trust to care for her… trust to care for her son. Knowing the gift was precious, he held her gaze as their bodies moved as one.

Waves of ecstasy overtook her once more and she cried out her release. Seeing the pleasure on her face unraveled the final thread of his resolve and he followed her as his own orgasm pulsed from his cock. Thrusting over and over, until every drop was gone, he drew in a ragged breath, managing to fall to the side to keep from crushing her.

The understanding that this was different, she was different, they were different, caused his arms to jerk as his heart pounded an uneven beat. Grinning, he pulled her body close, tucking her tight against his warmth. Kissing her gently, they lay, arms and legs tangled, until he finally slipped out to take care of the condom.

Sylvie watched him walk out of the bedroom, admiring his ass and muscular back. Her gaze drifted to the tattoo on his shoulder, a detailed drawing of a lighthouse in black and grey with perfect shading to give it a photographic quality. The golden beams of light coming from the top were the only color to the tattoo. Beautiful...just like the man.

After finishing in the bathroom, Mace stopped in the doorway, suddenly filled with uncertainty, not knowing if Sylvie wanted him to stay or leave, considering David was upstairs.

The slight ache between Sylvie's legs only added to the sated feeling she was experiencing. Smiling as she relaxed deeper into the pillow, she caught the expression of rare uncertainty on Mace's face as he walked back from the bathroom.

Assuming the cause of the concern, she sat up in the bed, her arms held out, beckoning. His face gentled into a grin as he stalked over, sliding under the covers and tucking her against him again.

"Are you sure?" he asked, holding her close. "With David upstairs, I can leave and there's no—"

She shushed him with a kiss, soft and gentle. Whispering against his lips, she replied, "You're right where

I'd like you to be. I'm sure you'll have to get to work before he wakes anyway, so we can have our night."

She snuggled closer and said, "I love your tattoo."

He shifted and held her gaze, drawing his finger over her cheek. "I wanted to ask you if you'd let David get one—a temporary tattoo, but like this one?"

Her brow knit and, even in the dark, he could feel her concern. Explaining, he said, "There's a miniature tracer embedded into the light of this tattoo. All the Keepers have it in case one of us is on a mission that goes awry and we need to locate them."

Her mouth formed an O, but no words followed as confusion still flooded her eyes.

"I'd only have David get a temporary tattoo but, with your permission, we could add a tracer to him as well."

Gasping, her fingers tightened on his arms. "You think he's still in danger—"

"Whoa, baby. Don't get ahead of me. I think that I want to do everything I can to make sure he's safe. Planning upfront is the best way to ensure that."

Letting his words penetrate, she nodded slowly. "He'd like to have a tattoo like yours," she admitted, "but, is it safe? Will it hurt?"

"I'm only talking about a temporary one. It'll be drawn on, not tattooed into his skin. And the tracer will be minuscule. He won't feel it, I promise."

Her eyes held his, gaining strength from him. "Okay," she agreed. "I trust you to take care of my son."

He nodded against her lips, ease filling his chest. Lying in bed with his arms around her, taking her weight as sleep claimed her, the sound of her breath soothed him. His lips curved in a slow smile as the feeling of peace descended. Whatever this was...wherever it was going...he did not want to be anywhere else but in this bed, with this woman, for as long as she would have him.

"What have we got?" Mace stepped off the elevator and into the compound, already seeing several of his men at work. He knew he was not late, but even with the extra minutes lying in bed with Sylvie, he hated to leave her side.

Josh grinned, saying, "I found their servers. Looks like we hit the payload last night. Members, donors. I'm going to finish analyzing what we've got before you decide what you want to do with the information."

"Cross reference it with anyone who might have had a connection to Charles Jefferson or the Crossover Building Company."

"You got it, boss."

"Any idea who Jonathan Adams is?" he asked.

Clay responded, "Been looking at the security feeds that we tapped into. Atkins didn't have anyone come in at that time, but he did go to lunch. Looks like he had reservations at Bella's—"

"Oooh, swanky," Babs called out, her fingers flying over her keyboard, her head barely visible over her laptop and piles of papers on her desk.

"Found it," Josh called out. Spinning around in his

chair, he grinned. "Jonathan Adams is a real estate agent. He owns Adams Realty."

"What's the connection?" Drew asked.

"Don't know, but I found a social media site that had Jonathan, Doug, and Richard playing golf at a tournament."

Nodding, he said, "Good work."

Calling it into Roberto, he looked over at his group and smiled. "I'll let the State Police do the official questioning. Anyone up for another nighttime reconnaissance?"

Cheers resounded and he laughed. Desiring to leave the official investigation, with all its constraints, to the State Police or FBI, he knew his band of rescuers preferred the subterfuge of slipping in during the night.

Babs called him over to sign invoices and as he leaned over her desk, he caught her staring at him. Her face broke into a grin and she said, "Looks like you and the pretty Sylvie finally got over dancing around each other and decided to do some dancing under the sheets."

Blinking in surprise, he opened and closed his mouth a couple of times. She laughed, winked, and took the papers from him. "Good for you. Both of you."

He watched her walk away, her step light, arms full of envelopes to mail. Hands on his hips, he dropped his chin to his chest, warmth gliding through him at the thought of Sylvie. Turning, he was shocked to see his men all grinning back at him. "Get to work," he groused, but could not keep the smile from his face.

18

"Are there really pirate caves around here?"

Horace smiled at the wonder on David's face. "Yes, indeed. Some of them had great names like Black Sam Bellamy and Dixie Bull. I'm sure you've heard of Blackbeard."

His eyes widened and his gaze shot out toward the water. Holding on to the side, he watched as Horace moved the boat through the water, keeping them well away from the rocks while not too far out either.

"Can you teach me sometime?"

Horace looked back at him, his body hidden behind the bright orange life jacket, but his face earnest with desire.

"How to steer the boat?" Horace clarified.

Nodding, he grinned. "I like how you make us go where you want to by turning the handle on the motor."

"No time like the present," Horace proclaimed, indicating for him to slide next to him.

On shore, Sylvie stood in the backyard, the breeze blowing her hair about her face and her arms wrapping closer to her body. She stared intently at the boat bobbing in the waves and her heart was torn between joy that her son was getting to experience something new and exciting, and fear for his life if the boat suddenly toppled over.

Arms came from behind and she yelped in surprise before recognizing the massive, tanned muscles that wrapped around her.

"Hey, babe," Mace whispered in her ear. "You were so lost in thought you didn't even hear me come out."

His warm breath tickled her neck and she leaned her head back against his chest. "I'm keeping an eye on David."

Mace lifted his gaze, seeing Horace and David out in the motorboat. "Worried?"

"Always."

"He'll be fine. Horace is an old sea dog...a former Navy SEAL."

Nodding, she remained silent, but breathed a sigh of relief.

"Was everything okay this morning?" For several nights, he had slipped into her bed once his work was completed. And every morning he had slipped out just as quietly, so that David would not see him.

Nodding again, she smiled. "Everything except you being gone when I woke."

Groaning, he agreed. "I'd give anything to wake in your arms." Nuzzling her neck again, he grinned as his lips felt her shiver. "Wake...and other things in the early morning."

She laughed as she turned in his arms, lifting her hands to his face. Rubbing her thumbs over his dark stubble she sucked in a deep breath. "You are so gorgeous." After the words left her mouth she quickly blushed.

He watched her lower her eyes and ordered, "Oh, no. You can't say that to me and then look away."

She rolled her eyes, then admitted, "I'm sure it sounds stupid, but sometimes when I look at you, I can't believe you're real." Seeing his surprised face, she added, "You're larger-than-life, Mace. Gorgeous, strong, everything I would think a hero would be."

He dipped his head so that he could stare into her eyes. "I'm no hero, Sylvie. I'm just a man."

"Not to me. To me, you're a hero. You're my hero."

His face gentled as he observed her staring so intently into his eyes. Closing the slight space between them, he kissed her lips, reveling in the soft, satin feel and her delectable taste. Reluctantly pulling away, he said, "If anyone here is gorgeous, it's you."

Just then, a shout from the water caught their attention. "Hey, Mom! Mr. Hanover!"

They turned in unison and observed a jubilant David waving in their direction. They laughed and waved back, but Sylvie said, "Oh, Lord, I hope he doesn't try to stand up." She felt Mace's chest rumble as he chuckled.

"Stop worrying, babe. He'll be fine."

She twisted her head to look up at him again, and

asked, "Is it crazy to think that he's safer on a little boat in the ocean than he is in our own home?"

Mace sobered, reaching up to cup her cheek again, knowing how much she worried about her son. "I won't let anything happen to you, or to him."

She sucked in a deep breath and smiled, offering a slight nod. With a last glance at the boat, now coming toward shore, she said, "Marge brought stew and buttered soda bread. I told her that I could cook, but she just told me that I needed to take things easy."

"She's used to doing things her way...best to just let her."

Laughing, she asked, "Interested in some lunch?"

"You know the way to my heart," he laughed.

As they walked into the house together, Sylvie could not help but wonder if his heart was already as involved as hers.

Lunch, as always, turned into a time of good food, fellowship, and laughter. David, well behaved, was still a typical little boy and his antics kept them in stitches while his questions kept Mace and Horace on their toes.

Marge could not hold back her grin as she watched Mace interact with both Sylvie and David. As the meal finished, Mace announced that he needed to get back to work. Ruffling David's head with promises to come back early that evening, he bent toward Sylvie, placing a quick kiss on her lips. Jerking, he suddenly realized the act of endearment had come so easily to him, but was the first time he had made such a move in front of anyone else. Staring at her shock-widened eyes, he blinked. For a man who prided himself on his control and quick thinking, he had no clue what to do.

Sylvie's eyes jumped first to David's face, seeing him nonplussed and smiling. A quick glance around the table gave evidence that Marge and Horace were equally pleased.

Mace, deciding to not make a big deal of his gaffe, shot her a wink before standing and saying, "I'll see you later."

She watched him amble out of the house and, for a second, wanted to disappear along with him. Unable to do that, she turned and faced the trio still at the table. Horace and Marge stood, clearing off the plates and moving into the kitchen, leaving her alone with David.

"Sweetheart, what you saw, was… well, it was… I suppose, that you could say—"

"Mom," David grinned. "It's okay with me if you and Mr. Hanover like each other. I think he's great. He's big and strong and he's nice to you. Not like…"

Her breath caught in her throat as his voice trailed off. She realized all the years of trying to shield David from Ed's bitterness and threats had not worked. While she had managed to keep Ed out of their lives, for the most part, his visits for money and threats to take David away had been witnessed.

"He's a great coach. And, I think he'd make a great dad," David added, his face turned up toward hers, hope burning in his eyes.

"Oh, honey. Mr. Hanover and I are not anything like that right now."

Grinning, he laughed. "I know how it works, Mom.

You're just dating right now." He jumped up from the table, grabbing his plate to take it into the kitchen, and said, "It's okay, you know. I'm just letting you know that if anything does happen between you two, it's okay with me." He trotted off into the kitchen, leaving her sitting by herself.

Blowing out her breath, she shook her head at the intuitiveness of her son and, with thoughts of both he and Mace filling her mind, a slow smile curved her lips.

Mace slipped through the dark halls, his night vision goggles easily giving him the sight necessary to make his way stealthily toward the office. Behind him, Bray followed, just as easily. Neither of them spoke as they made their way into the office of Doug Smiteson in the Crossover Building Company's headquarters.

Bray immediately headed to the computer on Doug's desk. Opening the laptop, using the information sent to him by Josh back at the compound, he had no trouble getting into Doug's files. Within a few minutes, he was able to send back to Josh the complete contents of everything on the computer. With a little more work, Josh would have been able to obtain that himself, but Mace liked the old-fashioned reconnaissance that came from being inside someone's space.

He moved to the filing cabinet and pulled out all the paper records on the building where Charles Jefferson had been attacked. Digitally scanning them, he placed them back as he found them. Walking past the credenza behind Bray, he perused several photographs. One appeared to be Doug's family, with a wife and two boys but, more interesting, were two other framed pictures. One showed a group of men, some in business suits and some in hard hats, and he recognized Richard Atkins next to Doug. Taking a picture of that, he sent it to Josh to identify the other people. The next framed photograph showed Doug with several other men and women, all professionally dressed. He would not have thought much about it except that one of the women was Eileen Jefferson...Charles' wife. Sending that to Josh as well, he turned back to Bray, observing as he closed the top of the laptop.

Gaining the all clear from the others in the van outside, they exited the office as clean as they had entered. Once in the van and headed back to the compound, he called Josh.

"Pull up anything you can find on Eileen Jefferson. Just found a connection between her and Doug Smiteson."

"Do you figure she knew anything about what was going to happen to her husband?" Tate asked, the assigned driver for the night.

"She's a real estate agent and Doug owns a building company. She was conveniently in Hawaii the night her husband was attacked. Might be nothing more than coincidence, but I'm sending it to Roberto."

Closing his eyes as the van continued down the road, he felt as though they were getting closer to the threat against David. But just as that thought hit him, he wondered what would happen when the threat was removed. *Will Sylvie and David go back to their life? And will I have a place in that life?*

A knock on the door startled Sylvie and she wondered if she would ever get over being so jumpy. Peeking out, she sighed in relief, seeing Babs. Opening it, she welcomed the woman in.

Babs, as usual, got straight to the point. "Look, Sylvie, I don't want to stick my nose in anyone else's business, but the last time I was here, you mentioned that you weren't sure about going back to your old job when your leave was up."

Motioning for Babs to follow, she walked into the living room and they settled into chairs. "Yes, that's true. The job is going nowhere and, after what happened with David, I know my boss wants to get rid of me more than ever. He sees a single mom as a liability and not an asset." Sighing, she added, "After this, I probably won't have a job to go back to at all."

"You're an administrative manager, right?" Seeing her nod, Babs continued, "So, I assume you do things like filing, typing, invoices, scheduling, all the stuff that has to happen to keep the business running, right?"

Nodding again, she asked, "Yes, but what is this about?"

"Look, Mace has no idea that I'm here mentioning this to you and I can't make any promises, but his business has grown and I'm overwhelmed with work. You're right here, looking for something to do. It just seems like the two of us could come up with an idea on how you can help...at least until you figure out what else you want to do."

A spark of interest flamed inside of her, but she wondered how this would work. "It sounds really interesting, Babs, but I have no idea how Mace would feel about that. I can imagine that what you work on is all confidential and I don't know that he would want me looking at that side of the business. And as far as he and I go..." she lifted her hands out to the side as she shrugged her shoulders.

Babs sighed and nodded slowly. "Yeah, I wondered if that would be a problem. I mean, personally, I think you're great for him and he seems to be really good for you and David too."

"Oh, he is!"

"How about if we just keep this conversation between the two of us for now and I'll see if I can sneak in the suggestion to him." Grinning, Babs added, "Then, if he agrees, it was his idea."

David's eyes never left his upper arm as Rank carefully drew the Lighthouse LSI tattoo on him. "You make it look so real," he enthused.

Rank had shown him his tattoo before they got started and David insisted he wanted one just like it. As Rank added the letters LSI to the base of the lighthouse, David grinned, careful to not jiggle his arm.

Sylvie stood nearby, watching with fascination at

Rank's talent and smiling back at her son. Mace, standing with his arm around her shoulders, nodded as Rank shot his gaze up to him.

Releasing her and stepping over to David, Mace said, "Rank is going to use a tiny bit of glue to adhere the tracer to your skin. It won't hurt, I promise."

David's grin never left his face as he looked up at him. "I can take it, even if it does hurt, Mr. Hanover. I wanna be tough like you."

"Son, you're plenty tough," he laughed, nodding toward Rank, who affixed the tracer to the center of the lighthouse light.

"There," Rank said, sitting back after ruffling David's hair. "You're all done."

David bounded from the chair, rushing over to show Horace, while she sucked in a deep breath. The sight of her son's beaming face was priceless. Turning toward Mace, she offered her silent appreciation with her arms wrapped tightly around him.

"Roberto, what have you got on Eileen Jefferson?" Mace asked.

"I interviewed her. She works for Jonathan Adams, who owns Adams Realty."

With Roberto on speakerphone, Mace looked over toward Josh, who was sending information to the screen. As he viewed one of the pictures he had taken the night before in Doug's office, he could see where Josh had identified Jonathan Adams standing next to

Eileen, on the other side of Doug. Josh then flashed the other photograph on the screen, that showed Jonathan Adams standing with Doug and Richard Atkins.

Mace said, "We've got a connection with her, through her employer, to the man who owns the building where her husband was assaulted and with the man who her husband was investigating."

Roberto replied, "I agree that she's a person of interest, but she was out of the area at the time and we've dug up nothing on her that indicates she was party to her husband's murder. They've got children, a typical house with a mortgage, enough life insurance to pay off the mortgage and the kid's college tuitions, and some left over for her to be comfortable, but definitely not to make her a suspect for murder."

He sighed. "Yeah, I hear you. She wasn't listed on any of the NSEG's lists, but I will say that her boss, Jonathan Adams, has my suspicions, since he is connected with both Doug and Richard."

"Agreed," Roberto said. "I'll be interviewing him today."

Ending the phone conversation, he stood and walked over to his computer, each of his men working at their own desks. He glanced toward Babs and noticed her pile of work appeared to be even higher on her desk. Standing, he walked over and looked down at her.

"You doing okay, Babs?"

"Just buried as usual, boss." She leaned back in her chair and heaved a sigh that puffed her short bangs up in the air. "Don't suppose you've thought of hiring someone else to help out around here, have you?"

Rubbing his hand over his stubbled jaw, he said, "I know we talked about it a while back but, I confess, I've been so busy lately, I haven't thought about it again."

"Well, if you do think of somebody or decide to interview, that'd be good. It would need to be someone who's got a background in administrative work…you know, invoices, filing, typing, scheduling, ordering… hell, even logistics." Shooting him a slight smile, she turned back to her work, her head bent as her fingers flew over the keyboard.

He moved back to his desk, but as he stared at his computer, an idea formed in his mind. Sylvie was an administrative manager and he knew she did not want to go back to her job. *I wonder…*

So deep in thought, he missed the smiles passed among his other team members as several of them winked at Babs.

19

Mace sat on the delicate chair in the living room of the Jefferson home. Concerned with the sturdiness, or lack thereof, of the furniture, he focused his attention on the well-coiffed woman perched on the edge of the sofa. Her clothes appeared expensive and she looked more like she was going to a business meeting than sitting in her house being interviewed by the police. He noted her complexion was pale and even her carefully applied makeup could not hide the dark circles under her eyes.

"I can't see that one thing has anything to do with the other," she said in answer to Roberto's question about the timeline of her conference and her husband's subsequent death, her pale hands clasped tightly in her lap.

"How long have you worked for Adams Realty?"

"For almost two years. I met Mr. Adams at one of Charles' election fundraisers. I had been in real estate many years ago, but took time off when our children were young and I felt like Charles needed me at his side. As our children left for college, I began to look for employment again. Jonathan Adams said he thought I would be an asset to his company and could work for him at any time."

"And the conference you attended?"

"I was thrilled to be able to go. Jonathan was originally slated to go to the conference but, at the last minute, was unable to. He said he had another obligation and the conference had been paid for, so he asked if I would replace him. Charles had no problem with me going, so I thought it would be good for my career."

Mace watched as tears formed in her eyes and she blinked quickly. Her fingers were linked so tightly in her lap, her knuckles were white. Sucking in a ragged breath, she said, "I had no idea when I left for the conference that I would not see Charles again."

"Mrs. Jefferson, as State Attorney, your husband had several open cases that he was working on. One of them was getting ready to prosecute a known hate group that goes by the name National Supreme Endeavor Group. Have you ever heard of it?"

She shook her head, her eyes clear as she stared at Roberto. "Not with any specifics. I have certainly read about them in the newspaper and I know that Charles was working on a case and had mentioned that group. But for the most part, he kept his cases private, as he should have."

"What about their leader, Richard Atkins?"

She startled at the question. Her brow crinkled, she cocked her head slightly to the side.

"I've heard that name, but didn't associate it with anything that Charles was working on. I think that Jonathan might know Mr. Atkins." She lifted a pale hand and rubbed her forehead, giving off a delicate sigh. "I'm afraid my memory is rather muddled right now, but I think I remember Jonathan once talking about playing golf with his friend, Richard Atkins."

The rest of the interview gave little information and soon he and Roberto were driving away. Looking to the detective next to him, he asked, "Did you notice the pictures on the mantle?" Roberto shot him a questioning look so he continued, "She had the same picture on her mantle that Doug Smiteson had in his office. One of her, Doug, Jonathan, and several others. There was also a framed picture of Charles standing with several men. One of those men was Richard Atkins."

"I wonder how long he might have known Richard? Before he ran for State Attorney or after?"

"You do your digging and I'll get my men on it."

Richard sat at his desk, his posture easy but, to anyone who knew him, the glint in his eyes was anything but casual.

Thomas Perdue sat in a chair to the side, sweat pouring down his back, trying, and failing, to hide his nerves from showing on his face.

Jonathan Adams and Douglas Smiteson rounded out the quartet.

"I want that kid," Richard said, his voice cold and words clipped.

"I tried—"

"And failed miserably." He shot Thomas a withering glare. "You stupidly showed up at his school and now have an entire office of people that can identify you."

Thomas grimaced, but remained quiet.

Turning his attention to Douglas, he asked, "Did you take care of the man?"

Douglas squirmed in his seat, loosening his suddenly too tight collar. Bobbing his head, he said, "Yes, yes. The worker who helped Thomas get rid of the body is gone. Paid off and sent back to Mexico with his family."

At the mention of Mexico, his eyes narrowed. His dislike for the country was well known among his cohorts at NSEG, but was equally as well hidden to the public. "You should have—"

"No, no," Douglas insisted. "Two dead bodies would have involved someone else to do the dirty work. It's better this way."

No one spoke for a moment, then he looked at Jonathan. "Get me any information on that kid's parents. I want them neutralized."

"I'm already on it," Jonathan bragged. "Seems she's a single mom. A neighbor took a fake package for her and said that she's gone on an extended vacation. Couldn't get anything else out of the old coot, but at least we know she's not in the house."

Glowering, he was about to explode, when Jonathan continued quickly. "I also found out her ex-husband is not in the picture, but is down on his luck. Man can't hold down a job. He'd be a good shot at trying to get to the kid."

For the first time since the meeting started, Richard settled back in his chair. A slow smile curved his lips and he nodded. "Well, done. Well, done. You managed to get Charles' wife out of town at the right time and you're proving to be invaluable to me here." Shooting his gaze to Thomas, he dismissed him, saying they had other business to discuss.

Thomas made a hasty escape, glad to be out of the viper's den.

As the door shut behind him, he looked at Douglas. "Get rid of him." Then, looking at Jonathan, he added, "And get me that kid's dad."

Once more, Roberto and Mace sat together, this time facing Charles' assistant, Steve. The young man appeared haggard with his hand-combed hair and his tie slightly askew.

Looking at the two of them, he apologized. "Sorry… things have been crazy around here since Charles'… uh…" He blew out a deep breath and looked away for a moment. Visibly gathering himself, he gazed at Roberto and shrugged. "Sorry."

Roberto dropped his chin in a sign of understanding, and said, "Take your time. We realize this is difficult for you."

Nodding, Steve agreed. "I was very fortunate to get this position. My dad always told me that many deals were made while playing golf, but," he shrugged, "I don't play golf. I work hard, don't have much of a social life, and was able to devote all my time to Charles' campaign. When he was elected, I was thrilled, but never expected to be hired as his assistant. I have a pre-law degree, but have to save money before I can go to law school. Charles giving me this job was a huge bonus to my plans."

"You mentioned deals made while playing golf. Was Charles much of a golf player?"

"He played, although I don't know how well. I know there were some charity tournaments that he would play in, just for the publicity and because he enjoyed giving back."

Mace leaned forward, holding out his phone, showing one of the pictures taken from Douglas' office. "Do you know if he had a professional or personal relationship with any of these men?"

Steve took the phone from his hand, staring at the picture intently, his brow furrowed. "Oh, yeah. Charles hated this picture and was furious that it showed up in the newspaper. One of the men in the picture was someone that he was investigating."

"Can you tell us which one that was?"

Giving off a rude snort, Steve said, "It's this asshole, right here." He pointed to Richard. "That was the big case Charles had been working on. He had evidence that the group Richard is the head of has been laundering money through other businesses."

"And were you privy to the results of his investigation?"

Nodding, Steve said, "As his assistant, I sat in on most of his meetings. I know that he and the State Police were closing in on Mr. Atkins. His main focus in the investigation was the laundering of money through the Crossover Building Company. In fact, the owner of that company is right here, standing between Richard and Charles."

"And the other man?"

"This is the realtor that Charles' wife works for," he indicated, pointing to Jonathan Adams. "I've made dinner reservations for him and Eileen with Mr. Adams."

"Have you been contacted by anyone, other than through official channels, about what you might know?"

Rolling his eyes, Steve replied, "Hell, I've practically been sleeping here in the office, just to get away from the press. I've worked with the other detectives from the State Police and have given them copies of all the notes that Charles had amassed."

Mace asked, "Did you handle his appointments." Seeing Steve nod, he then asked, "I'm sure you've been questioned as to Charles' appointments that day. Do you have any idea why he did not list where he was going?"

Shaking his head, Steve said, "He was meticulous about keeping his schedule. He always said that as an elected official, he needed to be transparent."

"Do you believe, for any reason, that he would have been open to bribery?"

At that question, Steve's eyes opened wide and he shook his head emphatically. "I realize you didn't know

Charles, but you can believe me, he had more integrity than any man I've ever met. If he was meeting with someone and didn't write it down in his appointment book, he would've had his reasons. My guess is that his reasons would have been that he was doing more investigating."

A few minutes later, he and Roberto walked out of the building, climbing back into Roberto's SUV. The detective looked at him, and asked, "What vibe did you get from the assistant?"

"Gotta tell you, he's the most believable person we've talked to so far."

Pulling out into traffic, Roberto nodded. "Agreed." Just then, Roberto's phone vibrated. Answering, he listened for a minute, before growling, "You've got to be kidding me." Listening for another moment, he disconnected. Turning to him, he said, "The body of Thomas Perdue was just found. We need to swing by the morgue. One of my officers working on this case said he's been identified as one of the men in the photograph David took. That means he could be our murderer. And, I want to see if he might be the one who when to David's school."

Mace sat at the table with his staff, reviewing the latest information that they had. "Thank God David did not have to identify Thomas' body. We were able to make a positive ID using the picture from Sylvie's phone."

Rank said, "So, Thomas killed Charles and then had to be silenced."

"That'd be my guess. We know Thomas had worked for the building company and he was currently on the payroll as an assistant for the NSEG."

Blake, looking at his computer, said, "Thomas has had several large deposits in his checking account, going back over the last six months."

Eyebrows lifting, he said, "And Charles Jefferson had been the State Attorney for six months. Whoever was out to get him, has been doing so since the beginning."

"Richard Atkins?" Walker asked.

Nodding, he replied, "He's my guess. He's got the most to lose…the most money to spend…and the means to shove everything under the carpet."

"So where does this leave us?" Josh asked. "If the State Police are closing in, what does that say about Sylvie and David's safety?"

He scrubbed his hand over his face, feeling his heavy scruff and not remembering the last time he had shaved. Worry settled deep inside of him, thinking of how important Sylvie and David had become to him.

"The noose may be tightening around Richard's neck, but that can just make him more reckless. He strikes me as a man who doesn't like to leave any possible messiness. David is still the key witness to who the first man was that was talking to Charles."

"But David wasn't able to positively identify Richard as the other man," Cobb objected.

Nodding, he agreed. "Yeah, but Richard doesn't know that."

20

Sylvie dreamed she was floating on the water, her body gently rocking. As consciousness slowly took hold, she realized her body really was moving, but not because of water. Instead, Mace's warmth surrounded her as he nudged her legs apart from behind, sliding into her slick channel.

With one hand wrapped around her chest, his palm on her breast and fingers tweaking her nipples, Mace nuzzled Sylvie's neck, delivering kisses along her shoulder. He knew his scruff would abrade her soft skin, but she didn't seem to mind, shivering underneath him.

Sylvie slid one hand behind her, her fingers digging into Mace's muscular ass, urging him on. Taking the hint, he thrust harder and faster, the friction sparking flames. She felt her inner core tighten and just as she was about to beg for more, his hand dipped over her mound. His thick forefinger found her clit and circled the taut bud, pressing gently.

That was the last her body needed to hurl her over the cliff, waves of ecstasy pulsating throughout her core. His name left her lips, albeit muffled, as she pressed her face into the pillow to keep her sounds quiet.

Feeling Sylvie's body clench around his cock, her sex even slicker than before, Mace felt his resolve to hang on longer diminished. Increasing his pace, he thrust to the hilt and released into her waiting body. Soaked in sweat, his muscles squeezed tight, he continued to thrust until completely drained.

Holding her close as he slipped from her body, he knew he wanted her to stay in his life. Her…and David.

Just then, a knock on the door sounded, and David's voice rang out. "Mom?"

Jerking up, Sylvie's eyes opened wide as she stifled a gasp, whispering, "Oh my God, he got up before you had a chance to leave!"

His voice equally soft, Mace assured, "The door is locked, babe."

Leaning over to place a quick kiss on his lips, she smiled her thanks. To David, she called out, "I'll be out in just a minute. You go ahead and get dressed and I'll get breakfast started." She breathed a sigh of relief as she heard his footsteps patter back down the hall and the creak of the stairs sounding. Flopping back on the bed, she allowed herself another moment to be engulfed in Mace's his embrace.

He leaned over, latching onto her lips as he pulled her close. "Now, that's the way I like to wake up."

She lifted her hand, cupping his stubbled jaw, and smiled. "Me too."

His face now serious, he said, "You and I need to talk soon." Seeing her crinkled brow, he continued speaking as he smoothed the creased skin with his thumb. "We know this is going somewhere and we don't have to define it right now, but David deserves to know that we're together."

She nodded slowly. "You're right, he does. I just kept waiting for the right moment, but I don't know that it will suddenly appear." Climbing from the bed, she pulled on her robe. "He's a smart boy, though. He's already told me he'd like it if we were together."

Jumping out of bed, Mace followed her into the bathroom, dealing with the condom. Stalking over to her, with a pretend glared on his face, he asked, "And when were you going to tell me this?"

Suddenly uncertain, Sylvie said, "I guess I wasn't sure how you'd feel about it."

Wrapping his arms around her he lifted her chin with his knuckle, holding her gaze. "There's no guesswork about it, babe. I'm crazy about you…and crazy about David. I say, let's tell him soon."

She sucked in her lips but was unable to keep the grin off her face.

"I'll be out in a few minutes and he can see us having breakfast together."

Nodding, she turned to walk out of the bathroom, shooting a wink at him over her shoulder. "Perhaps you'd best put on some pants first!" Laughing, she darted out of the room before he had a chance to retort.

Mace hurried into the compound, his phone already at his ear. "Going to put you on speaker, Roberto. We're secure. Just me and my men." The Keepers all stopped what they were doing, turning their attention his way.

"I wanted to let you know that Richard Atkins has now been indicted for money laundering. We're using a lot of the evidence you gathered, showing the money links between NSEG and Crossover Building Company. Douglas Smiteson has also been indicted and it appears that he's going to sing."

He nodded, "Smart play. He was the weak link in the chain and I can see him rolling over on Richard."

"What about the murder charges?" Rank asked.

Roberto replied, "Right now, Richard has lawyered up, probably figuring that money laundering will be a much less severe problem to deal with than murder-for-hire. But, we are putting the pressure on Douglas, since Thomas used to be an employee of his."

"And Sylvie and David?"

"I know you hate to hear this, Mace, but we may still need them. We can provide protection—"

"No worries. I've got them," he said quickly, ignoring the nods from his staff.

Laughing, Roberto said, "I figured you did. We'll talk soon and, as always, thanks for your assistance."

He smiled, the weight on his chest loosening some. Looking around at the grins on the Keeper's faces, he said, "Good work. It's not over yet, but maybe the end is in sight." As the words left his mouth, he hoped that with the threat lifted he and Sylvie would be able to talk about where their relationship was going. *I want them with me...but does she want the same thing? Would she be willing to move here?*

"Go! Go!" David screamed, jumping up and down while clapping.

Sylvie laughed at his excitement, then shifted her gaze back out to the water. Sitting in lawn chairs, Babs on one side, Marge on the other, with Horace and David cheering to the side, she watched the impromptu competition.

"How often do they do this?" she asked.

Babs rolled her eyes and shrugged. "Fairly often. Mace likes to call it physical training, but every one of them were former military and competition runs high in them."

"Is there a name for what they're doing?"

Laughing, Babs said, "Well, it's hardly an Olympic sport and I don't think there are any set rules. It's a mash-up of kayaking, basketball, polo, and wrestling, so maybe kayabaskepolorestling."

Eyes wide, she was about to ask another question, when David looked over his shoulder at her. "I know the rules, mom. Mace taught me all about it. They have to try to get the ball into their nets while paddling their kayaks, and then shoot it through the hoop. He says the rules are that anything goes, so they can wrestle with each other trying to get the ball or knock each other over."

"Do they even know what they're doing?" she asked, as she observed the ten kayaks in the water below in what appeared to be some kind of epic battle with a couple of balls, nets, and paddles.

That morning was the first time that she had met all nine of the men that worked for Mace. It was obvious their camaraderie was genuine and she envied their tight bond. She chuckled at the memory of Babs complaining about the testosterone in the workplace. With all of the Keepers so handsome and athletic, the eye candy was almost overwhelming, but none of them held her attention. Only Mace. Whenever he turned his dark eyes toward her, the intensity of them almost burned, making her feel like she was the only woman in the world.

She continued to watch while laughter rang out over the waves and joking threats and shouts of cheating commenced. Unable to keep from laughing herself, she inwardly cheered as Mace managed to expertly maneuver his kayak between two of the others, snagging the ball and throwing it into the net. He lifted his arms into the air and, with a whoop, looked up the hill, his eyes locking onto hers. Smiling widely, she waved, thrilled to see him relaxed and happy.

Horace elbowed David, and said, "Keep on cheering for whoever you want to win!"

"That's easy. I'll always want Mace to win."

Horace winked at her while clapping David on the

back. Babs and Marge shared a smile with each other, before sharing their delight with her.

As the men paddled to the rocky shore, dragging their kayaks out of the water, the spectators moved to the outdoor tables. She and Marge pulled the covers off the food as Horace began pulling sodas and beers from the tub filled with ice. Babs greeted the others as they came up the path, falling into step next to Drew.

Sylvie turned, watching as Mace walked over the grassy knoll, water droplets sliding over his tanned muscles, appearing like a god rising from the sea. If they were alone, she would've traced each drop with her tongue, casting any other thoughts from her mind. Feeling a nudge, she jerked her head around, seeing Marge grin.

Mace brought up the rear, filling his lungs with fresh air, loving the warmth of well-used muscles. He looked up and saw David running toward him, a towel in his hands. Grinning his thanks, he took the towel and rubbed it over his thick hair before draping it over his shoulders.

"What did you think of the game?" he asked.

David looked up, his smile wide, and asked, "Will you teach me how to play?"

He placed his large hand on David's shoulder as they continued walking toward the house. "Absolutely. But first we've got to teach you how to swim, how to kayak, and most importantly water safety. Once you've got that, then you can join us."

David's pace slowed and Mace looked down seeing the young boy pondering. Before he could ask what was wrong, David looked up and asked, "Do you think Mom and I can stay here? I really like it and I can tell Mom does too. She's been a lot happier since we've been here and doesn't have to go to her awful job anymore."

Mace knelt down to David's level, turning his smaller body to face his. "I'd like for you and your mom to stay. She and I will need to talk about it but, no matter what happens, I'll teach you how to play our game. So, don't you worry. You go on and grab some food."

Thinking he had just provided reassurance to David's concerns, he was stunned when David threw himself at him, encircling his neck with his small arms. The hug was over almost as soon as it began, but his heart stuttered. He watched David run to the others, pushing his way into the line at the food table. Standing, he saw Sylvie staring at him, her hand pressed against her trembling lips as she blinked to keep the tears at bay.

Stalking over to her, he pulled her into his embrace and whispered in her ear, "It's okay, babe. Just a little male bonding." He thought those words would make her laugh, but instead he caught the sound of a slight sob. Guiding her away from the others for a moment, he lifted her chin and stared at her beautiful face.

"I'm sorry," she said. "It's just that he's never had a male to bond with. And I have to tell you, Mace, I can't think of anyone in the world I'd rather him bond with than you."

Humbled and unable to come up with an appropriate response, he let his kiss do the talking. Pulling her close, he moved his mouth over hers, his tongue plunging into her warmth. Reluctantly dragging his lips away from hers, he kissed her forehead. "Come on, babe. Let's go get some food."

Walking toward the tables, with her tucked tightly into his side, he caught the smiles headed his way and, with a light heart, returned them.

Sylvie stood at the top of the stairs, a gentle smile on her face as she listened to Mace telling stories of pirates, lighthouse keepers, and derring-do. She could not help but wonder about the man who was now in her life… and her son's life. Hearing the story come to an end, she walked into David's room. The expression on his face, as he gazed up at Mace, warmed her heart. Bending down to give him a good night kiss after Mace had left the room, she was surprised when David wrapped his arms around her neck and held her close.

"Mom, I really like it here. Do you think we can stay?"

She had always prided herself on her honesty and, as she gently laid him back in bed, her hand smoothing his hair back from his face, she said, "I don't know, honey. I just don't know what the future holds for us. We have all our things back at our house. And all your friends…" He sighed heavily and her words died on her lips.

His face fell for just a moment, then, he looked back up at her. "Even if we can't stay here, do you think Mace will still be our friend?"

"I hope so," she whispered. "I truly hope so."

"He promised he'd teach me water safety. I wanted to learn their game, but he said I have to learn to swim first and then learn about water safety. Then, I can play their game with them."

His voice held such hope, her heart ached. Kissing him goodnight once more, she stepped out into the hall, startling when she saw Mace leaning against the wall.

"Oh, I thought you went downstairs."

His intense, dark-eyed stare captured her and she stepped forward, lifting her hand to place it on his chest.

His voice rumbled from deep inside, and he said, "We need to talk."

She sucked in a quick intake of breath, as if an icy bucket of water was just poured over her. Settling her features, she offered a slight smile that did not reach her eyes. "Of course." Turning, she walked down the stairs in front of him, each step feeling as though she were walking toward an end.

Once downstairs, he reached over and linked his fingers with hers, guiding her to the sofa. Surprised at the intimate gesture, she sat down, steeling herself for whatever he might say. She watched as he settled his bulk next to her, one arm resting on the back of the sofa, his hand on her shoulder. His other hand remained linked with hers.

Mace had heard the uncertainty in Sylvie's voice as she spoke to David and knew he wanted no misunderstanding between them. Holding her gaze, he sucked in a deep breath, and began.

"I never told you that this house belonged to my grandparents." He observed her eyes widen in surprise, but continued, "It was smaller then, the rooms cozier. My grandmother used to make quilts and she draped them over every chair, bed, and sofa. My grandfather would sit by the fireplace, smoke his pipe, and tell me stories of days gone by. Pirates and brigadiers. Sailors and soldiers. Lighthouse keepers and rescuers. He weaved tales into all of our evenings and I cannot tell you how many nights I spent here with them, entranced, entertained, and thinking this was the greatest house in the world."

She swallowed, finding her bravery, and said, "Mace, I'm sorry David asked if we could stay here. He's just a little boy who doesn't understand—"

He shushed her and shook his head. "No, I think David understands just how special this place is." Shifting slightly so that his hand could move through the silken tresses of her hair as he spoke, he said, "One of the reasons I loved this place was because my grandparents gave me a respite from my own home. My dad, a dissatisfied and angry man, spent his days at work and his nights yelling or drinking. We weren't physically abused, not in the way that you're probably thinking, but he let us know every day that being tied down with family was not what he wanted. Which is its own form of abuse. My sister and my mom found solace in each other but, for me? I spent as much time here as I could."

Sylvie could not help but squeeze the fingers that were linked with hers, suddenly struck with the thought of a dark-haired, dark-eyed little boy, desperately needing attention and finding it in his grandparents' little house on the edge of the sea.

"One night, my dad finally decided he had had enough and he left. I haven't seen, heard from, or spoken to him since then. By then, my grandmother had passed away. I was around ten years old. My mom worked extra shifts, my sister got a part-time job, and we ended up moving in here. Grampa kept the downstairs bedroom, because of his rheumatism. Mom and sis shared one of the upstairs bedrooms, and I slept in the one that David's in now."

They were silent for a moment, Mace lost in his remembrances and she struck by the similarities between him and David. Knowing he needed more time to talk, she remained silent, but smoothed her thumb over the calluses on his hand.

"Of all the stories Grampa would tell me, I loved the ones about the lighthouse keepers and their bravery the most. In many ways, I suppose, I felt that Grampa had helped save us…certainly me, and it made an indelible impression on me."

She touched her fingers to his tattoo, unable to see it underneath his t-shirt, but having memorized it. "Lighthouse…your tattoo…and your business."

Nodding, he said, "After I got an Associates degree and joined the Army, I knew I wanted to go Special Forces. Worked hard, studied hard, did everything I could do, and it paid off. Years with the Army's elite allowed me to be a rescuer of a different kind." Grinning at the memory, he said, "Grampa said it was his proudest moment when he got to watch me graduate from Special Forces School."

Her hair slid through his fingers and Mace moved them upward to the back of her neck, still feeling the tension there. Rubbing slightly, he smiled as she closed her eyes for a second, her muscles relaxing under his ministrations. Watching as she opened her eyes again, focusing on him, he was struck once more with how right it was to have her in this house.

"God, I loved my team. We twelve knew each other's thoughts and movements. My captain, Tony Alvarez, now runs his own security firm, along with my former Medical Sergeant, Gabe Malloy and his twin brother, Vinny, and Jobe Delaro. Another member, Chief Warrant Officer Jack Bryant also runs a security and investigative business in Virginia." Sighing heavily, he added, "It was fucked to have to leave them the way I did. I never got to say goodbye."

"What happened?" Sylvie asked, her voice full of concern as her fingers continued to move over Mace.

"Got called out for a special assignment. Had to leave in the middle of the night. My team was given no information other than I had to be reassigned. Eventually they were told I'd been killed in action. There couldn't be any loose ends, you know. I officially no longer existed."

She watched the play of emotions cross his face but was unable to discern each one. "Do you feel guilty? Did you have a choice?"

Chuckling, he replied, "When you serve, you go where Uncle Sam says you go, no questions asked. So I did…continued serving, and met some of the men who now work for me now. But…it left a hole."

"And now? Now, that you are all civilians?"

"I recently reached out to Jack and, through him, to Tony." His brow furrowed as he added, "It was good to see him. Brought up a lot of memories…felt like I was finally able to do the right thing by him." After a quiet moment, he shook his head and focused back on her face.

"Tell me more about Lighthouse Security," she requested. "I want to hear more about you."

Reaching up to tuck a strand of hair behind her ear, he said, "Well, Grampa died while I was still in the service and he willed his house and his land to me. Mom and sis stayed here while I was overseas."

"Where are they now?" As soon as the words left her lips, her heart squeezed in her chest at the sight of pain settling in his eyes.

"Mom died several years ago. Cancer. By the time she finally made it to a doctor, she didn't last long." He shook his head, sadness settling over him, and said, "I'm not sure she ever really got over Dad leaving and then…" He lifted his hand from her fingers to scrub over his face. His thumb and forefinger pinching the bridge of his nose for a second before exhaling heavily.

"Sis, unfortunately, had a boyfriend that wasn't much better than Dad. She finally woke up to what kind of man he was and broke it off. I was overseas and had no idea how bad things had gotten. She moved to a new town hoping to get away from him, but he found her. He broke into her apartment one night and, in a drunken rage, hit her. She fell backward, hit her head, and died three days later from swelling on the brain."

"Oh, Jesus, I'm so sorry, Mace," she gasped, reaching out, clutching his hand again, holding it close. "I'm so sorry, I'm so sorry."

He blew out another long breath, swallowing deeply. "I was overseas on a mission, unable to be contacted at first. All I could think about later was that I was working for my country, rescuing others, and wasn't here to rescue my sister."

Quiet settled between them, comforting. After a moment, she stated, "This is why you rescue now."

Mace nodded, his attention no longer on his memories but on the woman sitting so close he could feel her breath wash over his face. "Yeah. When I got out, I determined to do everything I could to keep others safe. With our reputation, we get some very high-profile cases. But, for me, helping people who have no other avenue of help, is what I love."

The desire to touch him was overwhelming and Sylvie reached up to run her fingers over his forehead before sliding them into his hair. Slowly dragging them downward she cupped his jaw, her thumb running over his thick scruff. Holding his gaze, she said, "I understand, Mace. I really do. Rescuing is not just what you do... it's who you are. I'm so grateful that you came to help David and me. I'm also grateful for the opportunity to share this house with you, for a little while, knowing that when the need is over, we'll leave. Please don't be bothered about what David asked...in a little boy's mind, he doesn't understand that this place is just a reprieve."

"No, babe," Mace insisted. "That's what I'm trying to tell you. This is *my* house… not a safehouse." Seeing her confusion, he explained, "I mean, yes, this is a safe place for you to be, but it's not a safehouse. I've never brought anyone here before you. Not a rescue. Not a woman. You and David are not here because I had nowhere else to put you. You and David are here because this is where I want you to be."

He chuckled, watching understanding slowly ease her worry lines. "Now you're getting it, sweetheart. I told you that we are at the beginning of *us*. And that us, includes David as well. So, when we're sure the danger has passed, I'd still like you to be here with me."

Exhaling a long breath, she nodded slowly. "I'd like that too, Mace, although first, I have to get my life back on track." He cocked his head to the side and she explained, "I need to think about a new job…David's school and friends. I want the start of us to be based on real life…not my fear or need to be rescued."

As much as he hated to admit it, she was right. Sucking in a deep breath, he nodded in agreement. He barely had time to brace as she suddenly threw herself at him, her arms wrapping around his neck tightly. He fell back on the couch, her body plastered on top of his, his arms banded around her middle. She moved her head just enough to latch onto his lips, all of the emotion she was feeling poured into her kiss.

Their tongues tangled, vying for dominance, as they devoured each other. Sylvie's breasts swelled and she felt the evidence of Mace's impressive need against her stomach. Grinding herself on him, she grinned as he groaned into her mouth.

He knifed off the sofa, her body cradled in his arms and stalked to the bedroom down the hall. Shutting the door with his foot, careful to not let it slam, he reached behind and pushed the lock button.

"Looks like someone wants to have their wicked way with me," she teased, her own eyes dark with lust. Her hands went to his belt, fumbling in their haste. Jerking his pants and boxers down, she sucked in a quick breath.

He lifted an eyebrow in question, but she curled her fingers around his massive erection. Moving her hand up and down his silky-hard shaft, she felt tremors move through the rest of his body and grinned at the heady power she felt. He allowed her to push him back onto the bed and she straddled his legs. Her lips moved over the tip, swirling her tongue around the sensitive head.

All rational thoughts dissolved into a lust-filled dream as Mace watched, and felt, Sylvie work magic with her mouth on his cock.

Continuing to slide him deeper into her mouth, Sylvie slowly pumped the base with her hand while sucking on the top with her lips. Occasionally grazing her teeth over his flesh, he would hiss and jerk his hips upwards.

He growled suddenly and, with a swiftness that belied his large body, he flipped them so that she was no longer on top, but flat on her back.

"I come, I come in you." He ripped the condom

wrapper, but she recovered from her surprise quickly enough to take it from him. She rolled the latex over his cock, anxious to feel him deep inside of her.

Once sheathed, he flipped them back and said, "Baby, you do whatever you want as long as you're on top and in control."

Strangely shy, she bit her lip in hesitation. "Um…any particular way?"

He laughed as he shook his head. "You on my dick, in any position you want? Hell, Sylvie, that's a man's dream come true."

Smiling, she lifted up slightly, placing the tip of his cock at her entrance. Slowly she lowered herself onto him, allowing her body to stretch as it fit his girth deep inside her wet channel.

Mace fought to hold himself still, the desire to plunge upwards and take over almost impossible to hold back.

Finally, fully seated, Sylvie glanced down at Mace's tortured face and a giggle slipped out. His eyes jerked open with a pretend glare.

"Never laugh when you're riding a man's dick," he warned.

His comment only made her smile wider. "I'm sorry, but you look like you're in such pain."

He bucked his hips upwards and said, "Get moving, baby, and you can take my pain away."

She lifted on her knees, sliding up before plunging downward quickly, eliciting a moan from her and a hiss from him. Finding a rhythm, she rode him, reaching deep inside to the secret place that craved the friction only he could provide.

Mace watched Sylvie's long, dark hair fall forward, cascading about them. Her full, rosy-tipped breasts bounced as she lifted and plunged. His fingers grasped her hips, guiding her movements.

She began to tire and leaned forward, placing her hands on his shoulders. Seeing her fatigue, he took over, plunging upward while holding her hips in place.

He could tell she was close and as she bent forward, he captured one of her nipples in his mouth, sucking and nipping. She threw her head back as the orgasm ripped through her, sending jolts to every extremity. He followed closely, thrusting as deep as he could reach, until every drop was poured into her.

She flopped onto his chest, her slight weight barely causing a grunt to escape his lips. She started to slide off his body but he clamped his arms tighter, holding her in place.

They lay for several minutes, sated and neither willing or able to speak. As consciousness slowly dawned, Sylvie was aware of one of Mace's hands tracing soft patterns on her ass while the other hand rubbed up and down her spine. The movement was soothing, giving her already relaxed body a sense of weightlessness.

Finally, lifting her head, she watched as his lips curved into a grin.

"Hey," he whispered, his eyes never leaving hers.

"Hey, back," she replied, her grin matching his.

"You okay?"

"I'm perfect," she confessed.

"Yeah. Yeah, you are." He sighed, adding, "I don't want to move, but I gotta take care of the condom."

She allowed him to roll her to one side before he rolled to the other and moved out of bed. Disappearing into the bathroom, he quickly came back and crawled under the covers with her.

Before losing her nerve, she said, "I'm on the pill." Seeing his wide eyes, she rushed, "You're the only man I've been with in eight years—"

"I'm clean," he interrupted, "and can show you the test results. But, if you want, I can get tested again—"

"I trust you."

Mace stared into her eyes, once more humbled by her trust. Enveloping her in his arms, cradling her head on his muscular chest, they lay for several minutes, neither saying a word, just letting the blissful afterglow move across them.

21

"That's fucking good news, man," Mace said, speaking to Roberto on speakerphone a few days later in the compound.

"I thought you'd like that. So, as it stands right now, Thomas Perdue has been identified as Charles' murderer, based on DNA from skin that was under Charles' fingernails. When Thomas dumped his body, he didn't bother to remove any traces of their altercation. Thomas' body also had scratch marks on it, with Charles' DNA. As to who murdered Thomas, the evidence is piling up that it was Douglas and my guess is that it was directed by Richard. The NSEG is facing indictments for money laundering, fraud, and whatever else the acting State Attorney can throw at them."

He grinned as the other men around the room smiled in victory. "Anything else on the others?"

"Douglas Smiteson is also being indicted on money laundering. Thanks to the help of your guys, our forensic accountants were able to discern how Crossover Building Company was laundering the money for the NSEG." Chuckling, Roberto added, "Faced with a long jail sentence, Douglas is starting to sing about Richard. It seems that Richard likes to blackmail others to do his dirty work and he had Douglas lure Charles to the building site, where Thomas was waiting for him."

"Good work, Roberto. As I said earlier, that's fucking good news."

"I won't say we couldn't have done it without you, but you made our job a lot easier. Until next time, take care."

"Looks like you can breathe easier now, boss," Tate said.

He nodded, but admitted, "Gotta tell you, I feel a helluva lot better knowing the threat to David is over."

"Send the bill to the governor?" Babs piped up from the side. The group laughed and he simply nodded in response.

Wrapping up the loose ends, they looked at the new assignments coming in. As the others worked, he leaned back in his chair, his mind firmly on Sylvie. With Thomas Perdue confirmed as Charles' murderer and Richard and Douglas indicted, David was no longer a threat to them. Sylvie and David would get their lives back. Lifting his hand, he absentmindedly rubbed his chest, his normally organized mind racing with all the possibilities…and problems. *David likes the house now, but what about a new school? New friends? What about Sylvie's work? A new job?*

Jumping when Babs walked over for him to sign a

stack of forms, he looked up as she bent over and whispered, "Slow down, boss. You can't figure out your whole new life in a few minutes."

Chuckling, he said, "Does it show?"

"Only to those of us who care."

Casting his gaze around the room, he saw the Keepers staring, smiles on their faces. Pretending to grumble, he started to move from the room as Babs took a phone call. She motioned for him to wait and he turned back to her.

She nodded before looking up at him and saying, "Senator Whitson? Conference call in an hour?"

Agreeing to the time, he made his way back upstairs for lunch, seeing Sylvie standing in the kitchen with Marge. Crossing the space quickly, he placed a quick kiss on her upturned lips.

"Hey, what are you doing here?"

"I got a call saying that David had some items at school that we needed to pick up. I didn't think about there being any work, gym uniform, or even artwork that he would have taken if he'd gone for the last day of school." Shrugging, she added, "I don't think there's anything very important, but he said he has an art portfolio that he really wants to keep. Did you need us for something?"

"Yeah, I'm glad you're here. I wanted to tell you Charles' attacker was positively identified as the man whose body they just found."

Her breath left her body in a whoosh and he held her close. He smiled at Marge and Horace over her head. "There's more, baby." He waited until she leaned back and stared up at him. "Two men who were involved have been indicted."

This time she sucked in a quick breath. "So, it's over?"

Smiling, he placed a quick kiss on her lips, aware of their audience, and said, "The threat is over."

She gave a little jump, bumping his chin, and squealed just as David came bolting into the room. Settling back down on her heels, she twisted her head and said, "David, we can go to the school to pick up your supplies."

"And home? Are we going home?"

His heart dropped at the excitement in David's voice. Taking Sylvie's hand in his, he gently pulled her around to look at him, his brow lowered. "Home?"

Her face gentled and she replied, "Our belongings are there, Mace. He's not anxious to leave here but his toys and books are there. My clothes." Emitting a little snort, she added, "I don't even know what's now growing in the refrigerator."

"Are you coming back?"

She looked down at her feet for a few seconds before lifting her eyes back to his. "Mace, I want what we have started and yes, I want to be here. But, I also have to figure some things out. I need to go to my workplace… hell, I might need to find a new job. I need to—"

"I've been meaning to talk to you about that." He looked down into her eyes, seeing a spark that he had not seen since meeting her. Sucking in a deep breath, he wanted to talk to her about something that had struck him the other day when he realized how much Babs needed assistance but, looking at her face, he knew this was not the time. She and David needed to get their life back on track—he just hoped he was going to be part of that track.

Marge declared, "I've got to go shopping, so how about we drive all the way to your place? Your car's there, so you can go to David's school afterward." She walked out of the kitchen, calling over her shoulder. "I'll get my purse and tell Horace to bring the SUV around."

Looking up at him, Sylvie said, "I know it sounds crazy, but as much as I love this place, I'm dying to go to a grocery store."

Sucking in an uncertain breath, Mace said, "I'd feel better if I were taking you. I've got a conference call, but I can let them know—"

Her face softened and she pressed her fingers to his lips. "I need to get David settled back in his house, with his things." Lifting back on her toes, she said, "This isn't the end of us, Mace. But, it gives us a chance to start over…as a normal couple, not in the middle of a murder investigation."

Kissing her once more, he knew she was right. "Any chance I can convince you to go on a date with me? A real date?"

Her smile blinded him as she replied, "I'd be honored to go on a date with you."

She and David walked to the SUV, and he watched as Horace and Marge got everyone settled. Waving as they pulled down the lane, he rubbed his chest, already missing them.

Standing on her front porch, Sylvie hugged Marge, tears prickling her eyes. "I don't know how to thank you for everything."

"Oh, hush," Marge shushed, her strong arms holding her tightly. Leaning back, she peered into her eyes. "Now, don't be a stranger. I've loved getting to know you and Horace is already suffering David withdrawal!" Sobering she added, "Mace will miss you."

Her lips curved into a slight smile. "I really like him, Marge. But, now that this is all over with and he can go back to his life, I don't know…" Her words trailed off, the idea of Mace no longer wanting her once she no longer needed his protection too painful to speak.

Marge narrowed her eyes and shook her head. "I've known Mace for years and can tell you, unequivocally, that man does nothing without careful consideration. He's head over heels for you and David, of that I'm sure."

"I'll see if we can come back on the weekend, once I've figured out what I'll be doing. I'm pretty sure my boss has already fired me, but I can see."

"Are you heading off to the school now?"

"Yes. I got a message that said I should come this afternoon. David is anxious to get his art pad back."

With final hugs, Marge trotted to the SUV while she and David went inside their house. He spent several minutes running around his room, reunited with his favorite toys and books. "Mom! When we go back to

Mace's house, can I take my video games? How about my…"

She stopped listening to the many items he rattled off, instead focusing on the idea of taking their possessions to Mace's house. Blowing out her breath, she tried to think of how to explain to David that they needed to take things slow.

She headed into the kitchen, where she threw out containers of moldy and old food. "Sweetie, we'll need to go to the grocery store after stopping by your school," she called out, "so let's go now."

Pleased to be driving her own car again and with David buckled into the back seat, she headed down the road toward the school. Pulling up to the front, she noted how different schools appear in the summer when no students are around. The playgrounds were empty and so was the parking lot. Glancing at the clock on the dashboard, she hoped she was not too late to pick up his things today. Together, she and David walked hand-in-hand toward the front door. Pulling on the handle, she realized it was locked. She pulled on the other door handle, noting the same.

She glanced down at his droopy face, shaking her head sadly. "I'm sorry, David. We must not have gotten here in time. It looks like they're already closed." Seeing him about to protest, she said, "But don't worry, we can come tomorrow. I'm sure your art pad will still be here then."

Walking back to the school parking lot, there was an old pickup truck, with a shell canopy on top, that was not there before. Unsure if it might be another parent wondering if the school was open, or maybe a school employee who left something behind, she slowed her steps to see if she could recognize the driver. As they drew closer, she observed no driver in the vehicle and did not see a driver anywhere around either. Shrugging, she focused on David as he hopped over the cracks in the sidewalk.

"How about we hit the grocery store and you can get whatever you want to eat. In fact, for dinner, we can even get takeout hamburgers."

He immediately perked up at the thought of fast food hamburgers. Turning his face up toward hers, he grinned. "With french fries?"

Laughing, she held her hand out for him to take, and nodded. "Absolutely. Can't have hamburgers without french fries."

He had just passed the age and weight for not needing a booster seat, but she still had one in the car that she had him use. He looked at her from the corner of his eye, the silent question passing between them.

Shaking her head, she said, "Let's get through the summer, David. Once you're a little taller and a little heavier, we'll get rid of the booster seat for good."

Nodding his acquiescence, he looked over her shoulder, his attention snagged, and his eyes grew wide. Before she could turn to see what he was looking at, a blinding pain exploded against the side of her head. Her son's scream was the last thing she heard.

22

Mace sat at his computer, entering the information needed to begin a new mission he accepted after his phone conference with Senator Whitson, from Florida. The Senator's granddaughter was attending a Florida college and had become involved with a group that made the Senator nervous. He had confessed to him that, while he was open-minded, he also was older and wiser to the dangers that a young woman could encounter.

At first Mace wondered if the Senator was simply overcautious, but within a few minutes of the group's investigation, he shared the Senator's concerns. Assigning the case to Cobb, who had a knack for working with political figures, he looked at the time on his computer screen, sighing heavily.

He wanted to call Sylvie but knew that would seem ridiculous. They had only been apart four hours. *Is this what life is going to be like without them?*

Rank jerked around in his seat, and shouted, "Mace!" Gaining his attention, he reported, "You asked me to keep an eye on Sylvie's ex-husband. I have a tracer on his old truck and he's done nothing but go between a fleabag hotel, a couple of hamburger joints, and bars. I set it to alert if he moved to a different location outside of his normal pattern and just got a signal. Double checking it...yeah, he's definitely at an elementary school."

Ice ran in his veins, his words clipped. "What school?"

"South Cove Elementary."

"Fuck," he roared, his heart dropping to his stomach.

The others quickly reacted, each to their duties, shouting out their information.

"Pulling up traffic cams now."

"Searching his bank accounts."

"Locating Sylvie."

"I'm on David's location."

Swallowing hard, his thoughts scrambled and for the first time, he experienced complete blankness when it came to a mission. A hand on his arm had him jerk in response before looking down at Babs.

"Mace," she said, her voice quiet, yet firm. "You got this. You built this organization from the ground up, doing exactly this kind of thing over and over. This is no different, other than your heart is now involved. Put that aside for now. Work the mission." Her fingers dug into his arm, the slight pain jolting him as she punched out each word. "Work. The. Mission."

Blinking, he pulled himself up to his full, impressive

height, and nodded. Turning back to his crew, he growled, "Give me all you've got."

"Sylvie! Sylvie!"

The black fog slowly moved away and as she blinked her eyes open, albeit painfully, she heard Marge's voice as gentle hands smoothed over her face. Somewhere in the background, she heard Horace's voice, muffled words, as he talked to someone.

"We've got her. No sign of David. What's your ETA?"

"David!" she croaked, sitting up quickly, then immediately falling into Marge's arms, her vision swimming in front of her as her heart seized.

Horace slid his phone back into his pocket and bent over her. She looked up, his face ravaged with worry creases. "Mace and the others are on their way. We'll get him back."

His words, so strong and confident, as though set in stone, caused her to nod even though doubt snaked through her. "But, I don't know what happened. He looked over my shoulder and when I turned, I was hit." She looked at the bloodied cloth in Marge's hand and reached out to touch her bleeding head. Her heart threatened to pound out of her chest as fear clutched her heart. "I don't know who has him."

"Ed."

She stared blankly at Horace, her brow lowering painfully in confusion. Before she could speak, Marge, gently holding the cloth to her head again, explained,

"Mace didn't trust your ex and had one of the men keep tabs on him. Part of that, was to place a tracer on his truck. They noticed he was here and Mace realized you were here also. It was too much of a coincidence."

"Ed?" She felt stupid, with nothing else to say, but her still-aching head was unable to process the rapid information coming her way. "But…"

"Our guess is that he may have been contacted by someone wanting to get their hands on David. It's a moot point now, but I take it Ed isn't too bright. Or, maybe that someone forgot to tell him there's no reason now."

"Oh, Jesus, oh, Jesus," she chanted, struggling to lift herself up.

Marge held her down, shushing her. "Girl, you've got a bloody knot on the side of your head. You're not going anywhere."

As reality crashed in, she began to shake and tears fell readily.

Horace moved closer and got right in her face. "Sylvie, I know you're scared, but honest to God, Mace and the others will move heaven and earth to get David back. No one is better than they are."

"But how?"

"Don't worry about that. Mace got hold of us, told us to get here and that's what we did. Found you, called it in, and they're on it. Our job is to take care of you and yours is to let them take care of David."

They assisted her to stand, both assessing her. Horace looked at Marge and asked, "Hospital?"

"No," Sylvie all but shouted. "I want to go home and be there when David gets home."

Examining her head, now that the bleeding had slowed, he agreed. "All right. I'll inform Mace where we are."

As she sat in the back seat of the Tiddle's SUV, silent tears continued to fall. *Please, Mace...find my son.*

Jonathan Adams sat at his desk, looking up when his secretary knocked on his door. "Yes, Ms. MacArthur?"

"I'm sorry to disturb you, Mr. Adams, but there is a man out front that insists you need to see him. He's acting strangely, but will not leave. When I threatened to call the police, he just laughed and said that you would not like that."

Brow knit, he asked, "Did he give a name?"

"He just said that his name was Ed and insisted he had a small package for you."

His outward demeanor did not change, but his pulse rate increased. "Thank you, Ms. MacArthur. You may show him back." Looking at his watch, he smiled, adding, "And you may leave for the day. It's a lovely afternoon and I'll lock up."

"Thank you, sir. If you're sure, I'd love to go ahead and leave. I'll see you tomorrow."

He watched as she left, then gripped the edge of his desk as he stood, working to steady his breathing. Lifting his head, he smiled as Ed was escorted in and then offered a polite nod to his secretary. Ed opened his mouth, but he silenced him with his hand, calling out, "Have a nice evening, Ms. MacArthur."

As she left, they stood, silently, until they heard the front office door close. Turning on his visitor, he growled, "What the fuck are you doing here?"

Ed, his gaze jumping around, said, "I've got him. My kid. The one you said someone would pay to get their hands on."

His face reddened as he stared at the man in front of him. "You fool. You were supposed to let me know what you could do. Let me know if you thought you could get to him safely. You were supposed to scope things out to find him. Not fucking kidnap him and bring him here!"

Ed's eager expression contorted into a grimace as he stared back at him. "Well, I've got him. And I'm supposed to get paid."

"Not by me, you moron!"

"Then call whoever your boss is," Ed bit back, his fingers twitching at his sides before scrubbing them over his face. "I need the money!"

"The man you're referring to is in jail! There is no money…there is nothing."

Ed's face went slack, his breath leaving his body in a rush and he slumped into the nearest chair. "No money…but…but…I've got him."

"Then take him back where you got him. Take him back to his mother."

Eyes wide, Ed shook his head. "Back? I can't."

He grimaced as though in pain, and asked, "What did you do?" Immediately jerking his head back and forth, he growled, "No. I don't want to know. Just go and fix whatever you fucked up."

Drawing himself up, Ed bit back, "Not without some money. You don't provide, I go to the police and tell them what I was asked to do."

"I don't have that kind of money—"

"Get it!"

Pinching his lips, his chest heaved. "I can get you a couple of thousand dollars—"

"Do it!"

He sat down in his chair and opened a lower drawer, pulling out a locked box. Opening it, he counted out the contents…just a little over twenty-five hundred dollars. Handing it to Ed, he said, "This is it—all I have here. Take it and get out."

Ed eagerly snatched the money from his outstretched hand, nodding enthusiastically. He was almost to the door when he spoke again.

"What are you going to do with the kid?"

Rubbing his chin, Ed said, "Just leave him somewhere. Someone'll find him." With that, he turned and jogged out of the office.

Jonathan slumped over, placing his head in his hands, hating ever having met Richard Atkins…or dealing with the NSEG.

Parked in the back alley, Ed looked at his old pickup truck and grinned. Moving to the back, he stood in indecision for a moment. Opening the door, he saw David, hands still taped together with an old handkerchief used as a gag. Lifting him easily, he set him in the alley behind the realty office. "Don't worry…someone'll find you soon. This'll give me time to get away."

David's eyes widened in fright, but he stayed still. Relief at being out of the truck, flooded him.

Ed set David down next to a dumpster and looked at him for a moment. He hesitated for a second, mouth open to speak, then, simply shook his head and turned away. Climbing back into his truck, he drove away, never looking into the rearview mirror. He had money in his pocket and a few hours to get away.

David watched his dad drive off, a tear sliding down his cheek. One thought was able to penetrate his distress though—*Please let Mace find me and mom.*

23

The military helicopter landed at the airport, using special permits to access space in one of the hangars. Josh and Walker stayed behind to monitor from the compound and direct the mission.

Mace hopped down, stalking over to one of the two, black, tinted-windowed SUVs. Speaking into his radio, he said, "Talk to me."

"His truck was parked outside the Adams' realty for almost twenty minutes," Josh said. "Rank can now use his locater and find it. David's locater has him still at the realty office. He must have left him there."

"Status?" he asked, his throat threatening to close with unfamiliar fear.

"Easy, boss. His heart rate is slightly elevated but he's alive. He's not moving so I'd say he's restrained or locked in somewhere."

"Sylvie?"

"Still with Marge and Horace. They took her back to her house."

The others had gathered around and Rank nodded toward him as he worked his tablet in his hands. Looking over, Rank asked, "You want Ed or David?"

Without skipping a beat, he barked out, "David." Turning to climb into the nearest SUV, he stopped and looked over his shoulder. "But after I secure David…I get first dibs on dickhead. Save him for me."

The others grinned and nodded. "You got it," they agreed in unison.

Guided by the lighthouse location sensor attached to David's skin, the Keepers had no problem making their way to Adam's Realty.

"In back," Josh's voice came through Mace's radio. He hopped out of the SUV before it came to a stop, his feet barely hitting the ground before he took off running. Skirting the corner, he pounded the pavement, his heart stopping before his feet did as he saw David sitting in the dirt by a dumpster.

Forcing his mouth to not spew forth the curses he felt like howling, he dropped down on one knee and whipped out his knife, deftly slicing the gag and the tape wrapped around his wrists. "Hey, little man, I've got you now."

David flung his thin arms around his neck, his voice breaking as he cried, "Mom. He hit Mom!"

"Shhh, she's fine, I promise," he assured, keeping his

arms tightly around David as he stood. Unused to these types of emotions rushing through him during a rescue, he gratefully accepted Blake's hand on his back to steady his legs.

Cobb and Bray walked around the corner, a blustery man between them. The man's eyes landed on David and all blood drained from his face.

"Oh, Lord...I had no idea he left him here." Realizing he spoke as though he knew the child was there, he snapped his mouth shut.

Mace turned his fierce, narrow-eyed gaze upon Jonathan Adams, and said to Cobb, "Get Detective Martinez here. Tell him we've just found the link that they were missing."

Jonathan's eyes bugged out and he threw up his hands, shouting, "I'm not part of it! I didn't know what they were doing."

"You were told to send Charles Jefferson's wife far away on business, and you didn't think why that might be? You helped set things up between Richard Atkins and Douglas Smiteson. And now, you're party to the kidnapping of a minor. I'd say you and the police will have a lot to talk about."

Cobb turned back around, lowering his phone from his ear, a grin spread across his face. "We had Detective Martinez at the ready. He's already on his way."

Bray moved close to Mace, placing his hand on David's back. "Hey, buddy. Will you come to me for a few minutes and let me check you out?" David shook his head, his arms jerking tighter about his neck. "I promise, Mace will be right here with you."

Just then, two State Police SUVs pulled into the parking lot, Roberto jumping out and hustling over. Cobb handed Jonathan over to them, quickly explaining what they had found. Mace carried David over to their SUV, where Walker had the back door lifted. Turning, he sat down with David in his lap, shifting him around so that Bray could give him a quick evaluation.

Answering their questions, David told them that other than bouncing around in the bed of the pickup truck, he had not been hurt. Turning his face toward him, his eyes still filled with tears, he asked once more, "Are you sure Mom's okay?"

"I'll never lie to you," he promised. "Marge and Horace are with her. They say she's got a bump on her head, but she refused to go to the hospital, wanting to wait for you at home. We've let Horace know that we've got you, so she can rest easy."

"Can we go to her now?"

"Absolutely, buddy. There's nowhere else I'd rather be, than with both of you together."

Cobb jogged over, with Roberto in tow. Seeing they were about to leave, Roberto smiled at David before leaning in toward Mace.

"I know who orchestrated this," he said, his eyes shifting sideways to David. "I also know you plan on doing something about it. You gotta let the police handle this."

Mace shifted David again, getting him buckled into the backseat. Turning, he held Roberto's gaze. "I get what you're saying. And, when we find him, I'll make sure to give you a call."

Roberto stood with his hands on his hips, and sighed. "When? After you fuck him over? Man, you cannot fuck this case—"

"You have my word, when we get our hands on Ed, we'll give you a call. But, other than that, I make no promises on the shape he'll be in." Climbing into the seat next to David, he gave a curt nod toward Roberto, and the Keepers headed out of the parking lot.

Sylvie sat on the sofa, David's favorite bear in her hands as Marge kept a cold compress on her head. The way her stomach knotted, she was not sure which was worse…head or stomach. Her gaze followed Horace as he paced, his phone plastered to his ear.

"They made it to David's location," he said. "He's fine! They've got him and he's fine!"

A tear slid down her cheek as she sucked in a shuddering breath. "Oh, thank God!" Trying to stand, she said, "We've got to go. I've got to get to him."

Marge held her in place again, and said, "Don't you worry, Sylvie. If I know Mace, they're on their way here right now."

Horace nodded as he disconnected the call. "Yep, they're coming here. David isn't hurt, but I'm sure he's scared and wants his mom."

Fifteen minutes later she looked out the front window from the sofa, seeing a large, black SUV pulling into the driveway. Horace and Marge were standing at the front door, and she escaped from the sofa, her legs shaky underneath her. Pushing past them, she made it to the front porch just as Mace ran up with David. She collapsed and David rushed into her arms. Crushing him to her, she sobbed, rocking him back and forth as he burrowed deep into her.

Mace, landing on the porch floor with Sylvie and David, wrapped his arms around both. He knew she needed to be lying down, but her need to hold her son was greater. With both of them in his arms, their tears mingling with smiles, relief flooding throughout, he felt a sense of rightness that he had never felt before.

Leaning back slightly, he looked at the side of her head, the bloody, bruised skin already a dark purple. His rage renewed, but he checked it, shutting the anger down for the moment.

David held on to his mom, and asked, "He hit you. He hit you hard. Are you okay?"

Nodding, Sylvie assured, "Yes, baby. As long as I have you with me, I'm okay." She felt Mace's hand slide gently from her back, to her neck, to the side of her head. She shifted her gaze to him, wincing slightly as his fingertips touched the abrasion. Offering a wobbly smile, she repeated her words to him, "I'm okay. Having you both with me...I'm okay."

Marge stepped over, her hand laying gently on Mace's shoulder. "Let's get everyone inside," she encouraged.

Agreeing, Mace stood, assisting Sylvie to her feet, David still in her arms. Taking her weight, he ushered them inside, settling them on the sofa. Bray entered the house and caught his eye, offering a curt nod before walking back out of the room.

He kissed Sylvie's forehead, his lips lingering longer than necessary and mumbled against her soft skin. "I've got to go…there's more business to take care of."

Her eyes searched his and she asked, "You'll come back?"

A smile touched his lips, as his gaze moved between her and David. "Wild horses couldn't keep me away from the two of you." With a final kiss, and a squeeze on David's shoulders, he stood, shooting a steady look toward Horace and Marge as he walked back out the door.

David looked out the window as Mace and the others climbed back in their SUV and pulled out of the driveway. His brow scrunched, and he asked, "What does he have to do?"

Shaking her head, Sylvie said, "I don't know."

Marge hustled toward the kitchen, calling out over her shoulder, "I'm going to make some sandwiches and get some food in the two of you."

David, still curious, looked up at Horace, and asked, "Do you know where Mace is going?"

Horace just mumbled, "Retribution." As both she and David looked at him in confusion, he moved down the hall saying, "I think I'll go help with those sandwiches."

Pulling up to the old barn outside of town, Mace noted the

pickup truck with the shell canopy on top. The idea that Ed had bound and gagged his own son, before putting him in the bed of the truck, caused his blood to run cold. The only other vehicle in the area was the black SUV of his men.

The door to the barn slid open as he, Bray, Cobb, and Walker stepped inside. His eyes quickly grew accustomed to the dim, musty interior. Straw and sawdust were scattered about the floor and in the center was an old, wooden stool. Ed sat, tied to the stool, his eyes wide with fright.

Stepping closer, he looked down at him, disgust on his face. Without taking his eyes from the sniveling man in front of him, he asked, "Got them signed?"

"Right here, boss."

Rank handed him a sheet of paper and his eyes quickly scanned the contents. Seeing Ed's scrawled signature at the bottom, he shifted his gaze back to the man in the chair. "You understand what you signed? No contact. In any form. You relinquish all rights to your son."

Ed's head bobbed up and down as he swallowed audibly. "Yeah, yeah. I get it."

"Get him up."

Ed was quickly untied and pulled to his feet. His head jerked around as he tried to look at all of them before his gaze settled on Mace.

Mace's fist landed squarely on Ed's jaw, hard enough to knock him back on his ass without breaking anything. Standing over him, he looked down, his face full of fury. "That's for hitting the woman I love and kidnapping the boy I hope to call my own. If I ever see you, hear of you, or find out that you even so much as breathe the same air as them, I will make your life hell."

Stepping back, he growled, "Get him to Roberto."

Mace lay in bed the next morning, his arms wrapped around Sylvie. Tucked on the other side of her was David. At first, David had insisted on sleeping in his own bed, but it had not taken long for him to cry out in fear. Sylvie had opened her arms, comforting David, as he slid underneath the covers with them.

He had whispered in her ear that he would go sleep on the sofa, but she had clutched his arm shaking her head.

"No," she whispered back, her eyes pleading. "I want you here with us. Please."

Lying as the early morning light slipped through the blinds, illuminating the two people that had come to mean the world to him, he thought of how his life had changed. For the better.

Sliding from underneath the covers, he moved to the bathroom. Finishing his business, he stepped back into the bedroom just as David was climbing from the bed, rubbing the sleep from his eyes. David saw him and a wide smile split his face.

"Hey, buddy," he greeted, hoping he would not be upset at seeing him.

David blushed as his eyes slid over to his sleeping mother before returning back to him. "I'm sorry I got scared last night—"

In two steps, he was right in front of him, squatting so that he could look him in the eye. Placing his large hands on the small boy's shoulders, he said, "Never apologize for being scared. Truth is, I was terrified yesterday."

"You were?"

"Absolutely. Whenever you think someone you care about might be hurt, it's absolutely scary."

"You were scared for Mom?" David asked hesitantly.

His heart warmed as he answered, "I was scared for both of you, because I care for both of you." He tugged gently on his shoulders, pulling him in for a hug. "No matter what, I'll always be here for you."

"You'll let us come back to your home?"

Feeling David's arms tighten about his neck, he glanced over toward the bed as he heard the sheets rustle. His warm smile landed on Sylvie as she sat up in bed, her gaze pinned to them. He watched as she wiped her eyes before the threatening tears could fall, and she smiled, nodding in return.

Speaking to both of them, he said, "There's nowhere else I'd rather the two of you be, than home with me."

24

SIX MONTHS LATER

Looking up from her desk in the Lighthouse compound, Sylvie called out, "Drew! I need your report ASAP. Invoices have to go out tomorrow."

Drew had the good grace to blush, as he acknowledged, "I know. I know. I promise I'll get it to you before I leave today, Sylvie."

She fired a grin his way before winking at Babs, whose desk was next to hers. Babs laughed, saying, "Some things never change, even with the boss' wife riding his ass."

Finishing the invoice that she was working on, her smile never left her face. From the moment she awoke in her old bedroom with David safe and his arms holding on tightly to Mace, hearing him say that he wanted them to be together, she knew it was time to make a change. Turning in her notice at work, she had gone one last time to her old office to collect her few possessions and say goodbye to Jeannie. It felt great to tell Mr. Thomas to stuff it and watch him sputter in defense.

Standing at the large window, looking out on the unfinished construction across the street, she had sighed heavily. Hating what her son had gone through, she also knew that it led them to find Mace.

He had told her that he had been considering offering her a job with Lighthouse Security Investigations, but that had been secondary to him wanting her to be his wife. Proposing marriage to her and fatherhood to David, they had become a family.

She had insisted David talk to a trauma counselor, certain that confusion over his father kidnapping him and then abandoning him...again...would leave lasting emotional scars. Mace agreed, but after a few sessions, the counselor assured her that David appeared well-adjusted.

Mace had spoken to David at length about his own father and the young boy soaked up the stories, understanding that Mace was the kind of man he wanted to be.

A month later, they married at a small service at the base of the lighthouse, overlooking the ocean. Having had a big wedding the first go around, she wanted simple and Mace was more than accommodating. Her parents attended, along with Mr. Curtis and Jeannie. They stood in front of Marge, Horace, Babs, and the LSI Keepers, and pledged their love to each other.

Calling David up with them, Mace also made his

vow to David, promising that the paperwork to officially adopt him had already been submitted.

Now, months later, that promise had come to fruition and Mace was legally David's father. Having worried about him being in a new school and making new friends, she discovered her concerns were foundless. David integrated perfectly in his new surroundings, but spent most weekends working with Horace to learn how to swim and handle a small-engine boat.

The elevator doors opened and she startled out of her musings, watching as Mace stepped into the compound with Walker, his head bent as he listened. As always when he entered her presence, his eyes immediately shot to hers and his lips curved into a smile.

Walker headed over to his computer station and Mace strolled over to her desk. Settling his hip on the corner, he leaned over and whispered, "It's been months but I still can't get used to seeing you here, right where you belong, Mrs. Hanover."

Sylvie's wide grin warmed Mace's heart, but they were soon interrupted as Bab's called out.

"Boss, got your CIA liaison on the phone. You want it now?"

Lifting an eyebrow, Sylvie grinned. "Duty calls, sweetheart."

Kissing the top of her head, he acknowledged, "Put him on speaker, Babs," before turning to face the Keepers, ready for their next assignment.

Lighthouse Security Investigations
Mace
Rank (coming Jan 2019)

Heroes at Heart (Military Romance)
Zander
Rafe
Cael
Jaxon
Jayden (coming 2019)
Asher (Coming 2019)
Zeke (coming 2019)

Baytown Boys (small town, military romantic suspense)
Coming Home
Just One More Chance
Clues of the Heart
Finding Peace
Picking Up the Pieces
Sunset Flames
Waiting for Sunrise
Hear My Heart

Saint's Protection & Investigations (Military Romantic Suspense)
Serial Love
Healing Love
Revealing Love
Seeing Love
Honor Love
Sacrifice Love

Protecting Love
Remember Love
Discover Love
Surviving Love
Celebrating Love
Searching Love

Alvarez Security (military romantic suspense)
Gabe
Tony
Vinny
Jobe

Sleeper SEAL
Thin Ice

Letters From Home (military romance)
Class of Love
Freedom of Love
Bond of Love
The Love's Series (detectives)
Love's Taming
Love's Tempting
Love's Trusting
The Fairfield Series (small town detectives)
Emma's Home
Laurie's Time
Carol's Image
Fireworks Over Fairfield

Please take the time to leave a review of this book. Feel free to contact me, especially if you enjoyed my book. I

love to hear from readers!
Facebook
Email
Website

Made in the USA
Lexington, KY
11 November 2018